I STILL DO

CHRISTIE RIDGWAY

Silhouette®

SPECIAL EDITION®

Published by Silhouette Books

America's Publisher of Contemporary Romance

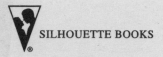

SILHOUETTE BOOKS

Recycling programs for this product may not exist in your area.

ISBN-13: 978-0-373-65432-1
ISBN-10:   0-373-65432-4

I STILL DO

Copyright © 2009 by Christie Ridgway

This edition published by arrangement with Harlequin Books S.A.

Visit Silhouette Books at www.eHarlequin.com

Printed in U.S.A.

"I'm not interested in meeting other women."

Will's voice was low, rough. Obviously she'd poked a sore spot. Emily might have laughed if he didn't sound so serious. "Okay. I understand."

"You understand nothing." Then he yanked her close again. "Or if you do, explain it to me. Because I don't understand *this*."

His mouth slammed into hers. The goodness of it made her gasp, and then that little bit of oxygen made it to her brain and made her wake up to what they were doing. He'd been waiting thirteen years to be a bachelor, to be heading out to parties and picking up women. So how was it that he found himself unable to resist the woman who was— just for the moment—his wife?

Dear Reader,

Quick. Picture your first love. Now, imagine meeting him again. You're both single, the sun is shining and the old magic between the two of you is sparkling like fairy dust in the warm air.…

This is the moment that Emily Garner and Will Dailey experience as they unexpectedly run into each other on the grounds of a Las Vegas resort hotel. And the magic doesn't dissipate as night descends. Instead, Emily and Will revel in the incredible feelings they have for each other, and two days later, buoyed by their emotions, they visit a little wedding chapel and take an impulsive gamble on each other.

But once back to real life these two have to face the consequences of their quick decision. After a lifetime of responsibility raising five younger siblings, Will was looking forward to bachelorhood. Emily's open to a new start and is eager to find love, but is "Wild" Will the right man for her?

First love becoming forever love is one of my favorite romantic themes. I hope you'll enjoy reading how Emily and Will find their happily-ever-after.

Best wishes,

Christie Ridgway

Books by Christie Ridgway

Silhouette Special Edition

Beginning with Baby #1315
From This Day Forward #1388
*In Love with Her Boss #1441
Mad Enough to Marry #1481
Bachelor Boss #1895
I Still Do #1950

Silhouette Desire

His Forbidden Fiancée #1791

Silhouette Yours Truly

The Wedding Date
Follow That Groom!
Have Baby, Will Marry
Ready, Set...Baby!
Big Bad Dad
The Millionaire and the Pregnant Pauper
The Bridesmaid's Bet

*Montana Mavericks: Home for the Holidays

CHRISTIE RIDGWAY

Native Californian Christie Ridgway started reading and writing romances in middle school. It wasn't until she was the wife of her college sweetheart and the mother of two small sons that she submitted her work for publication. Many contemporary romances later, she is happiest when telling her stories despite the splash of kids in the pool, the mass of cups and plates in the kitchen and the many commitments she makes in the world beyond her desk.

Besides loving the men in her life and her dream-come-true job, she continues her longtime love affair with reading and is never without a stack of books. You can find out more about Christie or contact her at her Web site, www.christieridgway.com.

For Rob, who took me to Las Vegas
and started me thinking of quickie weddings
and long happily-ever-afters....

Chapter One

Coming awake, Emily Garner rolled her head to the side, her cheek finding a cool spot on the scratchy material of her…pillowcase? Pillowcases weren't scratchy.

She wiggled her toes, encountering rigid confines. Sheets didn't usually confine her feet, either. Inhaling a breath, she realized she was still wearing that torturous strapless bra she'd borrowed from Izzy. The one with the underwire that made her lungs feel like an asthma attack in the offing.

Hmm. So she was still completely dressed. And, she realized, lying on top of a bed instead of in one.

Meaning last night she must have—*last night!*

Her heart jolted as last night—and what she'd done during its dark hours—flooded her brain. Eyes flying open, she jerked upright on the bed.

The blackout curtains covering the hotel windows gave the room a murky gloom. Sunshine peeked around the edges, confirming it had been hours and not mere minutes since she'd sat down on the bed after—

The bathroom door swung open. Emily's heart jumped again as a dark figure loomed in the doorway, backlit by golden light and the curling steam from the shower, like the headline singer in the Vegas show they'd seen last night before she'd…before they'd…

Oh, God.

"Will?" she whispered, her voice a croak. One hand pressed the bodice of her dress to her chest, while the other yanked at the hem of the spangly garment, another item from Izzy's wardrobe. "Is that…is that…?"

"It's your best friend." The husky voice of Isabella Caveletti—Izzy—sealed the identification as she stepped over the threshold.

Emily felt only slight relief. "It was all a dream, then?" she asked, voicing her foolish, foolish hope.

"Nope," Izzy said, walking between the beds. "It happened. And after we married the men, it appears we passed out on our new husbands."

New husbands. Emily mouthed the words as Izzy

threw back the curtains. The sun caught her full in the face and she slammed her hands over her eyes with a whimper. "What were we thinking?"

Behind the shield of her fingers she could sense Izzy moving around the room. "We were thinking it seemed like a good idea at the time," her friend answered.

Emily swallowed her next childish whimper, because, good God, she was no child. She was thirty.

But that had started it all, right? She and Izzy celebrating her step into the decade of the big 3-0 during an annual librarians meeting held every September. After two days amongst other bibliophiles who seemed as dusty and as boring as an outdated set of *Encyclopaedia Britannica,* Emily had agreed with her former college roomie and best friend that it was time for her to stop being the stereotype and start living a little.

And then two afternoons ago she'd bumped into Will Dailey, both on their way to the celebrated wave pool at the Jeweled Jungle Hotel & Casino. They'd never made it there—the chance meeting of an old friend was apparently enough turbulence for them both.

It certainly had set her world on end.

She dropped her hands and squinted at Izzy, who was frowning over her cell phone. "Oh, God, Iz. I didn't think we had all that much to drink."

Izzy shrugged. "We had enough. And that was on

top of four nights of no sleep, two because we stayed up so late catching up, and the next two because we found ourselves wined and dined by men who each rate their own month in a firefighters' charity calendar. I think we can justly claim that last night we were under the influence."

Under the influence of what, exactly? In Emily's case, sentimentality was part of the mix. Will was a childhood friend, the summer boy she'd loved from twelve to seventeen. And then there was that "live a little" promise she'd made to Izzy, not to mention the normal nerves a woman might feel on the brink of starting a new job—in the same county where Will lived. She'd been made giddy by all of it.

"Does this bring back memories?" Moving closer, Izzy held up her cell phone. On the screen was a photo of Emily and Will. They were laughing for the camera, squeezing each other tight. She looked exuberant, and he looked…

All grown up. Ruggedly handsome, with broad shoulders and chest, not to mention strong arms that had held her so close she knew the delicious smell of the skin at his throat. She sighed, and looked back at her own image. "I'd forgotten the veil."

"Remember? We rented them. But the wedding ring is yours to keep."

Emily's gaze dropped to her left hand. And at the sight of that shiny circle, she relived the whole evening all over again. The fun they were having, the crazy idea of honoring the old promise they'd made as kids to wed if they were unmarried at 30, the way that Izzy and Will's best friend, Owen, had leaped at the chance to be their attendants…and then the impulsive, dizzying decision the other two had made to marry themselves. The truth was, the couples had both egged each other into the idea.

When they had returned from the chapel, the women had wanted to dash upstairs to their shared room to freshen up, still running on a combination of alcohol, adrenaline and impetuosity. The guys— oh, God, their husbands—had said they'd wait for them at a table in the bar. "I was only going to sit down on the bed for a minute," Emily told Izzy.

Her friend nodded, flipping her phone closed. "Me, too. I couldn't find my lipstick, and I thought if I closed my eyes, I'd remember where I put it."

Emily now squeezed hers tight. "Okay, okay. We're in a bit of a jam, but Lordy, Iz, there's no one I'd rather be in a jam with than you."

"This isn't like appeasing the sorority's housemother after we forgot it was our turn to man the reception desk."

"I know."

Izzy was moving around the room again, but Emily had a teensy little headache, so she lay back on the mattress to think while she studied the inside of her eyelids. "But hey," she said. "The good news is that we always wanted to be the maid of honor at each other's wedding."

"We didn't think that through either," Izzy called from the bathroom. "How could we both be the maids of honor? You went first last night, so I was the maid of honor at yours, but you were the *matron* of honor at mine."

Matron. Matron? A married woman? That didn't feel real. And married to *Will*…well, the idea was the stuff of teenage dreams. When she'd seen the opening for the position in California's Ponderosa county, it had caught her attention because Will's hometown of Paxton was there. But when she'd applied for and later accepted the job, she'd never *seriously* thought of seeing him again. Not seriously. He'd dropped out of her life at seventeen, the last time they'd been together at summer camp in the Sierras.

Her thumb worried the gold circling her left ring finger. Besides that he was a firefighter, she still knew little of his life in the last thirteen years. But they'd had plenty of time to enjoy each other's company in the past two days. People watching at the hotel's pools, walking the Strip after dark, whooping it up with Izzy and Owen on more than one dance floor, though never stopping by the slot machines or the game tables. It hadn't seemed like they needed anything but each other to feel lucky.

But what were they going to do now? It was a true tangle, not only because she and Izzy had stood up the men—their *husbands*—the night before, but because Emily was well aware this wasn't some child's joke or college prank but an adult issue that the four of them were going to have to face head-on. Surely the men were having the same kind of cold-light-of-day second thoughts.

Will and Owen were both Paxton firefighters and Emily was moving to a town nearby, but Izzy consulted with libraries all over the country. Her stuff was scattered amongst friends from California to Connecticut, and Emily wasn't even sure she paid rent anywhere in between. It was hard to imagine Izzy settling in one place, let alone settling down...

But worrying about what Izzy was going to do was just an excuse not to think about her own life and what she had to face.

Thank God Izzy wouldn't let her get away with that. "I love you, Iz. I'm so glad you're here with me now."

Emily opened her eyes to look at her friend, who was standing beside the other bed, her suitcase stuffed full and zipped tight. Guilt was written all over Izzy's pretty, olive-skinned face and her brown eyes slid away from Emily's.

She jerked up again, now struck by the reason her friend had been so purposefully moving about the room and bath that they'd been sharing. "Isabella Caveletti, *what* are you doing?"

Izzy, chic as always, had on a sleeveless, black linen pantsuit and low heels with sharp toes spiky enough to serve as Cupid's arrows. "I—I have a flight out. You know that. I'm expected in Massachusetts tomorrow morning. The town of Lawton needs my help."

"*I* need your help. We *all* need help. For God's sake, we got married last night!"

"I can't deal with that right now," Izzy said, her face flushing. "I have a job to do, and…and…"

"What's Owen going to think? What's *he* supposed to do?" *What am I going to do?* Emily wanted to cry, but she was afraid if she finally released those words she'd fall completely to pieces.

"Owen will figure things out. You can give him my cell number…or, on second thought, don't. Tell him I'll call him. Soon. After this job is wrapped up. Or the next one."

Emily stared at her friend. She'd never seen Izzy flustered or panicked, not even when she'd attracted an outraged mob of librarians at the conference this week, the vocal group incensed by the sight of her prominent lapel button: "Dewey" with a red slash through it. Librarians clung to their decimal system tighter than a miser to cold, hard cash.

Speaking of hands…were Izzy's shaking?

Emily stood up from the bed and crossed to her friend. "Iz…" She rubbed the other woman's upper arm. "What's the matter?"

The brunette let out a trembling laugh. "Besides the obvious? That we got married last night? Do you…do you think there's a chance we can get the marriages annulled?"

Emily sighed. "I suppose. It's not like we, well, it's not like we had sex with them."

Izzy's shoulders slumped. "Right."

"What?" Emily narrowed her eyes. "Izzy…"

"Gotta go." In a flurry of movement, the other woman hugged Emily, snatched up her bags, and ran for the door. "Talk to you soon!"

"Izzy!" But Emily was left in the room with only the closed door and the framed notice that she had an 11:00 a.m. checkout time.

And the realization that she was all alone. Again.

The idea struck her hard.

All alone, like she'd been for the past eight months, since her mom, her only relative in the world, had passed away.

But instead of allowing the loneliness to well inside her, she focused her thoughts on the problem at hand. What was she going to do now?

The only answer that occurred to her was to follow Izzy's lead. But she couldn't do that, could she? She couldn't sneak out of the hotel, sneak out of Las Vegas, sneak out of Nevada.

Gathering together her resolve, she reached for the

hotel phone. She didn't have Will's cell number, but the hotel could connect her to his room.

He didn't pick up.

And he didn't pick up ten minutes later either, after she'd packed her bags.

All right, she bargained with herself. She'd try once more, and if she got no answer she'd leave a message. She practiced it out loud to get it right: "Will, Em here. Hey, I had to head out. Let's catch up in Paxton to sort through…things."

Her tone was bright. Perky even. Not a word reflected the turmoil she felt inside or the relief that she could postpone their inevitable showdown.

After leaving the message and hanging up the phone, she did as she'd wanted to all along. She did what Izzy had done and hightailed it out of town. Making a convenient leap of logic, Emily told herself that the car trip to California, in the company of all the belongings she was bringing to her new job, was the best way to figure out how to handle the fact that she was now married.

And to figure out why she'd gotten herself into such a mess in the first place.

For the first time in his life, Will Dailey wished he'd become a police officer instead of a firefighter. Then, he thought, marching toward the glass double doors of the county library, he could go inside with a pair of handcuffs and arrest the woman.

Emily Garner.

His wife.

The thought injected another acid shot into his stomach, which had been churning like a cement mixer since he'd discovered that the woman he'd married had checked out of her hotel room and ran out of Vegas, leaving only a cowardly—and too cheerful—phone message behind. He'd run himself then, but had been unable to track her down until today, almost a week later, which he'd been told was her first day on the job.

And his face was going to be the first one she saw, he promised with a grim smile. Then he pulled open the door and strode inside, determined to get the whole thing straightened out immediately. No damn retreating from the situation for him.

There she was.

Despite himself, he froze. Across the spacious carpet, her head bent over some papers spread on the reference desk, was the woman who had said "I do" five nights before, with a throaty catch in her voice and a wicked promise shining in her eyes. God, he'd had a thing for Emily Garner since the first time he'd seen her, when he was twelve years old.

He'd been new to the summer camp, his parents thinking—rightly so—that he needed some time away from his five younger siblings who stair-stepped the ages of two to ten. Emily had been the seasoned camper assigned to show him the ropes.

Then she'd worn her nut-brown hair in a pair of braids and had a mosquito bite on one tanned knee. He'd thought she had the bluest eyes in the world and he'd known he was going to have the best summer of his life.

There'd been five more just like that first one. Swimming, canoeing, archery. Campfires. KP. Emily laughing at his jokes, daring him to races, letting him steal a kiss when they were thirteen years old.

There'd been many kisses after that.

He'd gone on to high school and to excel in sports, especially the sport of flirting with girls—lots of girls. But the summers had belonged to Emily. He'd belonged to Emily. He'd worn the bracelet she macraméd and she'd put on his Paxton Panthers Football sweatshirt when the nights turned chilly. That last day of that last summer, they'd lain on their backs, shoulder to shoulder in the warm grass. With the scent of pine in their lungs and the sweet flavor of first love on their tongues, they'd daydreamed about the future. Their entwined hands had been sweaty, but neither one of them had broken their grasp as they promised to marry each other if they were still single by thirty.

He couldn't remember what had prompted the

conversation or what caused him to make the vow. Marriage hadn't been on his mind.

Only Emily.

But then he'd gone home and a tragedy one rainy September night had changed his life forever. No, not forever, he hastened to assure himself. As a matter of fact, he'd just recently gotten his life *back*. And no impulsive, impromptu Las Vegas wedding was going to return him to the box of endless responsibilities to others he'd been trapped inside for the last thirteen years.

Sucking in a deep breath, he allowed himself a few more minutes to observe her from afar. Maybe then he'd figure out how Emily had gotten under his adult, on-his-first-vacation-in-forever skin so fast that he'd done something as ridiculous as stand in front of an Elvis impersonator and say "I do."

She looked like an adult now too, in a little khaki-colored dress that was buttoned up to her chin and ironed within an inch of its life. Her shiny brown hair was too short to braid. It swirled around her heart-shaped face, with bangs that skimmed her straight brows and framed those startling blue eyes. Her nose was short, just like the rest of her, and her mouth looked soft. It *was* soft. Hot, too. He remembered—

"Wild Will!"

At the sound of the old nickname, Will jerked around to stare at a young man who looked vaguely familiar. He searched through his mental Rolodex. "Uh…Jared? Jon? Um…"

"Jake." The kid extended a hand and pumped Will's in an exuberant handshake. "I'm one of Betsy's friends. Pool party? I hit my head on the side and you drove me to the E.R.?"

"Oh, yeah." It wasn't the first time he'd had to play nursemaid to one of his siblings' friends. And it hadn't made much of an impression, as accustomed as he was to playing parent to his brothers and sisters.

"What's Betsy up to these days?"

"Graduated from college." He couldn't keep his grin to himself. His youngest sister, out of his hair and on her own. After thirteen years of worry, thirteen years of second-guessing his every move, thirteen years of pretending he knew what the hell he was doing when his siblings looked to him for security and support, he was finally free of family.

Free of care.

"She out of the house?"

"Yep. They're all out of the house."

Jake must have heard the relief and satisfaction in his voice because his smile widened. "Whoa-ho. You look like a man ready to make up for lost time. Now it's Wild Will's turn to play, huh?"

Wild Will. There it was again, that old nickname. The one he'd had in high school. The one he'd lived up to—to a point, anyway—because his summers belonged to Emily. He glanced over his shoulder at her, and saw that she was still frowning over the papers on the reference desk, oblivious to his presence.

God, if only he'd been oblivious to hers in Vegas. But their casual glances had met and they'd both halted their footsteps, stunned to see each other again.

He was still stunned. Of all the women in all the world to meet up with just weeks after he'd promised himself it was finally, finally his turn to fly high.

Only to fall flat on his ass by getting himself hitched instead.

"I've got a lot of living to do," he told Jake, though he was really reminding himself. "I've been tied down for too long."

"I hear ya, man," Jake said, laughter sparkling in his eyes. "But, hey, a library doesn't seem like the first place I'd go if I was looking for good times." His gaze roamed the room, then his eyes widened. "On the other hand, I don't remember the librarians looking like *that*."

Will frowned. "Looking like—"

The kid let out a low wolf whistle. "Maybe she'd let me check her out instead of a book."

Annoyed, Will shot a look Emily's way and then glared at Jake. He didn't know who made him more irritated, the woman for not appearing like a librarian should or the younger man for practically drooling over Will's wife.

Oh, God. His *wife*.

"Yeah," the younger man continued, rubbing his palms together. "I wonder what it would take to get her between the, uh, stacks."

"Listen, Jake," he heard himself grind out. Then his pager went off, saving him from making a fool of himself. He glanced down at the read-out. Groaned.

"What's the matter?"

"It's my captain. People have been falling like flies thanks to some flu going around. It's my day off, but now I've got to go in."

"Ah, too bad." Jake clapped him on the shoulder. "But cheer up. You'll get your wild on, I just know it."

Will turned toward the door, then gave a swift glance over his shoulder once more. Yeah, he was definitely going to get his wild on. Just as soon as he got that wedding ring off Emily's finger.

Chapter Two

The day after the "Firefighters' Flu" had left the station house shorthanded, Will returned to the library. He'd gone home for a shower and some sleep after his extra shift ended. The night had been a busy one and he didn't think it was smart to confront Emily without charging his batteries first. But now, wide awake after a second shower and two cups of coffee, it was time to get the ball rolling on their…breakup.

He yanked open the glass door and his gaze instantly found Emily—again at the reference desk, again looking incredibly sexy. But now wasn't the time to be thinking of that three-letter word, the one starting with an *s* and ending in an *x,* he decided with a grimace. Not when she looked so curvy and so damn appealing in a sweater that matched the startling blue of her eyes. And not when she was surrounded by a trio of teenagers clutching pencils and worksheets and gazing at her like she was a goddess.

"Ninety-five theses," she said, laughing. "Martin Luther posted ninety-five theses on the door of the church." Then she whisked her hands at them. "That's the last one. I'm sure your European History teacher sent you to find the answers at the library from books, not from the reference librarian."

"One more, *please,*" a boy pleaded, his strong build and football jersey making clear where he spent his Friday nights. "I have to be at practice in twenty minutes and if I don't get this done I won't have time later for my English reading."

Emily was already shaking her head, but then her gaze caught on Will as he approached the group. Her cheeks flushed and he saw her swallow. "Well, um, I, um, I suppose…"

"Ms. Garner always had a soft spot for football players," Will commented, coming to a stop behind the kids.

Her gaze darted to him again even as the tall high schooler grinned and glanced down at the paper he was holding. "Sweet. What's that other one we need, guys?"

"Who wrote *The Prince?*" the girl of the group piped up. "That's the last one."

Frowning, the other boy squinted down at his own worksheet. "I have that. It's the Marquis de Sade."

"Eww," the girl squealed. "It is not. The Marquis de Sade was the whips and chains dude."

The football player turned to eye her with new interest. "Amanda? How do *you* know about whips and chains? I bet you've never even been French kissed."

"I have too!" The girl flipped her straight blond hair over her shoulder. "I'll have you know that—" she broke off and slapped her paper against the now-laughing athlete's arm. "Brent Spier, you're nosy and annoying."

"And loud. All three of you are too loud," Emily put in, then lowered her voice. "The author of *The Prince* was Niccolò Machiavelli, and he's been given a bad rap, if you ask me. His name has come to stand for cynicism and unscrupulousness, when he was in fact bothered by the immorality of his age and was just writing about the political reality of the times."

But her short history lesson was completely ignored by the students as they quickly filled in the last blank on their papers—hesitating only to ask how to spell Machiavelli—and then they were dashing out of the library.

Leaving Will alone with his wife.

But now that he had her undivided attention, he

didn't quite know where to start. It wasn't cowardice, it was…something else that was causing him to hesitate. But damned if he'd let her think she had the upper hand on him. Crossing his arms over his chest, he told himself that today they were going to play things his way.

Still, he glanced in the direction of the teenagers' hasty retreat instead of rushing the topic. "Were we ever that young?" he asked, stalling.

She shrugged, her cheeks still pinker than normal. "Hard to imagine. But I'm pretty certain I didn't know anything about the Marquis de Sade at sixteen."

"But you knew plenty about French kissing."

Her face flushed again, and he didn't even feel bad about it, because God, thinking of Emily and French kissing had him heating up, too. The first time they'd kissed, he'd been too scared to do more than brush his lips against hers. It had been that way the several times they'd kissed at thirteen and fourteen. But the summer he was fifteen, following an experience that previous winter when an older girl had introduced him to a more European technique, he'd taken his kisses with Emily to a new level.

In Las Vegas, following that initial stunned moment of recognition, he'd hugged her first then bussed her cheek with his lips. But later that night, as they danced to something that had the sensuous beat of a languid pulse, he'd bent over her mouth and without a thought he'd touched her wet, hot tongue with his. In the space of that kiss he'd become aware of two things, one amazing—they fit together as if no time had passed between them—and the other crucial—that neither of them was a kid any longer.

They were now adults and he'd wanted to indulge like an adult.

But not get married!

Shaking his head, he stepped closer to the desk. It was time to tackle the subject. "What the hell were we thinking?"

Emily lifted her shoulders and spread her hands, apparently not needing further clarification. "I read they super-oxygenate the air in the casinos. Maybe we were kind of…"

"Drugged?" Because God knew he'd felt dizzy the entire time they'd spent together. But was that the casino's fault…or hers? Because when he'd realized he was still in Las Vegas but without Emily, the crash had come. Slam, bam, the realization had hit him, hard. Wild Will had done the stupidest thing a man who wanted to start living it up could do. "And then you ran out on me, Em. And Izzy on Owen. What the hell was up with that?"

She bit her bottom lip. "How *is* Owen? Izzy had some back-to-back jobs lined up she had to get to. But she promised to call him as soon as she could. Has, um, has Owen heard from her?"

"She left him a message, pretty much on par with the one you left for me."

Emily ignored the last part of his remark. "I'm glad she contacted him. She can be a little, um, hard to pin down."

"Unlike yourself?" he asked dryly.

She bit her bottom lip again, making it appear darker and wetter. "What can I say, Will?"

"You can tell me what you thought you were going to accomplish by leaving me hanging like that."

Her hands busied themselves with a stack of paper on the desktop. Then they moved on to straightening the pens and pencils in a nearby mug.

Understanding dawned. "It's the Danielle Phillips thing, isn't it?" he said, shaking his head. "It's the Danielle Phillips thing all over again."

Emily looked up at him, surprise written on her face. "I haven't thought of Danielle Phillips in years."

"But this is just like that. You used to avoid unpleasant subjects, hoping they'd just go away. Remember? You knew Danielle Phillips was stealing things from your cabin, you actually found your favorite necklace under her pillow, but it took you forever to do anything about it." Exasperated, he glared at her. "Damn it, Emily, you should know by now that some things have to be faced head-on."

"It was my favorite necklace because you'd given it to me."

Just like that, three-quarters of his bad mood evaporated. He'd brought her the necklace their last summer together as a belated birthday gift. It was nothing original—a sterling silver heart strung on a matching chain—but he'd agonized over it like no gift before or since. On the back he'd had their names engraved. Will + Emily.

He shook his head to dislodge the memory. He didn't want to be Will + Emily. He'd been Will + for the last thirteen years. Will + Siblings. Will + Responsibilities. Will - all that was what he wanted for himself. Now single Will sounded good. Unencumbered Will sounded even better. Wild Will best of all.

Surely Emily would understand that their quickie marriage needed to end with just the same amount of speed.

"Em…"

"Will Dailey!"

At the sound of the familiar voice, he squeezed shut his eyes, doing an Emily in hopes that the unpleasantness could be avoided. But he'd had thirteen years of practice knowing that whether it was a pile of dirty laundry or an empty gas tank in the family car, most things wouldn't go away on their own. He turned to confront his sister, Jamie, barreling down on him.

She had a toddler's hand clutched in hers. On her hip, the baby was chewing its little fist, and drool was running from the wet skin to collect on his sister's shirt sleeve. "You!" Jamie said, coming toe-to-toe with him. "In a library?"

Without a by-your-leave, she passed the infant over to him. He accepted the warm bundle—did he have a choice?—and remained stoic as Baby Polly started gumming his shoulder instead of her own fist. His nephew flung himself at Will's knees and wrapped around his legs like a parasitic vine.

"Todd," he said, wincing. "Be careful. The only toe-holds in Uncle Will's shins are the ones you dug into his bones the last time we were together."

Jamie's hands were free to be propped on her hips. "I'm so glad I ran into you. None of us have seen you in ages and I wanted to ask you something."

"No. I have to work."

She frowned, and brushed a strand of her boy-cut hair off her forehead. "When do you have to work?" she asked, a suspicious note in her voice.

"Any time you need me to babysit, or help build a fence, or assist in painting your family room."

"Will…"

That plaintive note in her voice was not going to move him. Didn't she get it? Hadn't she been listening? He'd made it clear to every single one of them that the minute his youngest sister was on her own he wanted to be on his own, too. He'd managed to avoid most of his siblings all summer. Ducking out of barbecues and Sunday dinners, and even one birthday party—his. He'd asked for solitude as his gift from the sibs.

Well, solitude of a sort. More than once, he'd gone out for beers with his buddies from the station and had spent the evening contemplating the joys of taking home one of the very lovely ladies he'd spotted at the bar. That he hadn't actually brought one back to his now-empty abode was beside the point.

"I'm busy," he reiterated, then kissed the baby on the top of her head and handed her back. Todd had already lost interest in Uncle-Will-as-tree and was sitting on the floor, accepting a picture book that the librarian was handing him.

The librarian. Emily.

"I'm *very* busy," he told Jamie, sending a sidelong look at his wife and sharpening his voice so his sister would get the hint. He had very busy business with Emily.

Jamie got the hint, all right. She glanced at Emily and her eyes widened, too. "Oh. *Oh.*" Her hand shot out. "Hi. I'm this guy's sister. Jamie. Jamie Scott. That's Todd, and the baby is Polly."

Emily shook Jamie's hand. "Nice to meet you. I'm Emily Garner. I'm Will's…"

Oh, hell. She wouldn't—she couldn't—his family would never let him hear the end of it if they found out what he'd done in Vegas. "She's my friend," he blurted out, with another meaningful look, this time shot at the librarian. "My old friend Emily from camp."

Jamie's eyes went even wider. "*Emily from camp?*"

Too late, Will remembered that he might have—a time or two—told Jamie about her. She was the next oldest after him, and they'd been close as teenagers. Later, he'd taken on a more parental role with her, but still, he'd confided in her on occasion. About Emily.

"This is perfect," Jamie gushed, bringing the hairs on the back of Will's neck to attention. "Say you'll come tomorrow night! It's just a little get together. I live only a couple of blocks away."

Will hastened to play wet blanket. "Emily just moved here not long ago—"

"All the more reason for her to meet some people, don't you think?" She turned away from Will. "What do you say, Emily? You've just got to come. You're going to come, right? Say yes."

"Um, well, um, okay," she said, looking a bit flattened by the steamroller that was his sister Jamie. "I suppose I actually wouldn't mind…"

"Then it's all set. Tomorrow night. Six o'clock. 632 Orange. Or shall we get Will to pick you up?"

Emily glanced over at him. "I can find it. And I think Will said he was working."

Jamie grinned. "We'll just see about that." She linked her arm with Will's. "C'mon brother. I need your help."

He pulled back. "I'm not done here."

She yanked harder. "It's Polly's car seat. I don't think it's strapped in correctly."

His eyes narrowed.

Jamie's big brown ones were as difficult to refuse as the long-lashed peepers the baby had trained his way. Manipulators, the both of them. "Fine," he grumbled.

The dimples in Jamie's cheeks dug deep. "Thanks. It will just take a minute."

It took fifteen. The car seat check was quick, but then he had to manfully pretend to resist her attempts to get him to agree to dinner at her house the next night.

Of course he was going to be there. There was never any doubt he'd let his wife run amok amongst his relatives, even though he was pretty certain Emily had gotten the hint not to spill those beans.

And there was still all their unfinished business— though it had to wait until the next day, because when he went back into the library he was told that Emily had left for an off-site meeting that would keep her from her desk past closing time.

It was easy for Emily to locate 632 Orange, a pleasant, rambling house with a lush lawn and a porch swing, but finding a nearby parking space proved to be difficult. She had to carry the Bundt cake she'd baked more than a block, which gave her stomach plenty of time to flutter with nervous anticipation. It wasn't easy for anyone to meet new people, she told herself. But these were *Will's* people. That made it worse.

And so much more interesting.

From his attitude yesterday, it was clear that he meant to sever their Las Vegas connection as soon as possible—what did she expect, after all?—so this might be her one and only chance to satisfy her lingering curiosity about him. How had he changed in the last thirteen years? A couple of fantasy days and nights of sunbathing and slow dancing hadn't answered all her questions. Learning more about the grown man that was once her summer boyfriend could help make it easier for her to leave him and their impulsive wedding behind.

The door of the house swung open before she could ring the bell. A dark-haired young woman stood on the other side, a woman younger than Jamie, but the familial resemblance was strong. "Emily," she said, smiling. The noise of a crowd reached over the threshold, and she raised her voice to be heard over it. "I'm Betsy, the youngest Dailey. Jamie told me to keep my eye out for you. I've been told I'm in charge of your good time."

As Emily stepped into the house, the clamor created from the combination of loud voices, rock music and splashing water grew louder. "I'll be fine on my own," she protested, even though her feet stuttered a bit as she took in the dozens of people attending what Jamie had called a "little get together."

Betsy shook her head. "You look shell-shocked already, and we haven't even started on the family introductions."

"Family?" Emily echoed. Surely this horde... "They can't *all* be family."

"Pretty much," Betsy confirmed, grabbing a soda from an ice-filled cooler and pressing it into Emily's slack hand. "In some way or another, anyhow. You know there's six of us, right? Six siblings. We're all supposed to be here tonight, not to mention other extended relations and their assorted spouses, significant others and charming children."

"Will said he came from a big family, but—"

She was cut off by a brief, but exuberant hug from Jamie. "You're here! Is Betsy taking care of you? Do you need something stronger than that soda? There's chips and pretzels on the deck in the back. Have you seen Todd?"

The last question was thrown at a man who was breezing past, a spatula in his hand. "Todd?" he repeated, as if the name was new to him.

Jamie narrowed her eyes. "You know, your son."

The man—presumably her husband—reached out to chuck her under the chin. "No worries, Charlie's got him." Then he turned a smile on Emily. "Hey. I'm

Ty. You're the newbie, right? Come on out to the barbecue when the Daileys start to make you nuts. I'm from a family of a mere five so I know how this tribe can get intimidating."

Emily had been an only child. Her parents only children as well. That this many people would be closely related to each other boggled the mind. How would she keep them all straight?

As Ty and Jamie wandered off in separate directions, she couldn't help from clutching Betsy's forearm. "Is… Is Will going to be able to make it?" And though she knew that didn't bode well for the future they *weren't* going to have together, she suddenly wanted to see him.

"Later, I think. He had to fill in at the station for half a shift. There's a bug going around. C'mon." She gestured toward the back deck where people were milling. "It won't take you long to get to know everyone."

Betsy was an optimist. There were so many people at the party and they were moving so fast and talking with so much energy that Emily had a hard time keeping up—not to mention keeping up with their names.

Betsy she knew. Jamie and Ty.

Charlie—Ty's brother—was the tall man holding the little boy, or was that Will's youngest brother, Tom? Tom was accompanied by his girlfriend,

Gretchen, who looked a lot like Betsy's roommate, Chelsea. Chelsea maybe had a thing for Charlie, though perhaps Emily just thought that because their names started with the same two letters.

Then there was a Jack, a Max, two Daves and a Patrick. Oh, and Alex. A couple of those were Will's brothers and others were former frat brothers…or something like that.

Besides Chelsea, there were other women she was trying to keep straight: an Ann, a Helen and two blondes whose names wouldn't stick.

That didn't even begin to cover the kids who were in the pool, crawling over a big plastic playhouse and propped in a playpen with plastic blocks.

Her head reeling, she took Ty up on his offer and escaped to the relative quiet of the barbecue he was tending. He glanced over at her. "Madhouse, huh?"

She held her cold, sweating soda can against her cheek. "I'm a librarian. I'm trying to check my impulse to walk around shushing everyone."

With an expert flip, he turned a sizzling burger. "Having second thoughts about accepting the invitation?"

Emily shook her head. "I recently made a promise to a friend that I'd try to get out from between the bookstacks and live a little. I definitely think this qualifies."

"Would that friend be Will?"

"No." She half-smiled, supposing that she and Will would never be friends now. Not that she could tell Ty about the marriage. It had been clear the day before that Will didn't want her talking about that. "Will's more of a..." She glanced up to catch Ty studying her more seriously than she expected. Her eyebrows rose. "Is something the matter?"

"Just curious about the woman causing Will to break his promise."

"Pardon?"

"In June, he told everyone not to expect to see him at any family functions for a good long while. And yet there he is now." Ty nodded toward the opening in the sliding glass doors.

Emily looked over. Yep. There he was. Her heart bumped against her ribs as she took in the sight of him. In a pair of worn jeans, running shoes and a T-shirt, he shouldn't look so special to her. But wasn't it natural to be fascinated by how he'd filled out in the intervening years? His shoulders were broad, his strong forearms dusted with dark hair, and there was the shadow of masculine stubble on the lower half of his face.

In Las Vegas, she'd shivered at the feel of the whiskery, erotic brush of it along her cheeks and neck. Her mouth had been abraded by it so many times as she kissed his jaw, that the second morning they'd met she hadn't needed lipstick—her lips remained reddened from the late-night caresses of Will's chiseled chin and mouth. Now, his gaze roamed the backyard and she slid hers away, averse to being caught staring. He wasn't hers to watch.

Ty's words echoed in her head. "Wait," she said. "Why would he promise to avoid family functions?"

"Because—"

A voice growled in Emily's ear. "Did this guy forget to mention he's married?" Will reached over to give Ty a good-natured punch in the upper arm. "You hound."

"Hey, hey, hey," Ty replied. "There's no call to be throwing names around. Emily just needed a breather from the Dailey-clan chaos. You of all people can understand that."

"Yeah, you got that right. But now I'm here. Emily, can I get you—"

"Will!" Betsy rushed up and grabbed him from behind in a fierce hug. "You never call, you never write."

He shook his head, and rolled his eyes at Emily. Then he turned to his sister. "Betsy Wetsy. I think you've grown a foot since I saw you last."

"Don't think you're going to make me mad with that dumb nickname." She grabbed one of his hands in both of hers. "You have to come out and see my new car."

"Bets…"

"You have to. I can't figure out how to get the

hood latch open. Aren't I supposed to check the oil or something?"

"Every time you get gas. Didn't I teach you that?" He was no longer protesting as she dragged him away. "Five minutes," he said over his shoulder. "Give me five minutes, Emily."

It was more than five. As she moved around the party, she followed Will's progress through his various siblings. There was Betsy's car issue. His brother, Max, wanted to show off his new cell phone. Alex issued a video game challenge that apparently couldn't be ignored. When it came time to gather around the long picnic tables that had been placed end-to-end on the grass below the deck, the youngest brother—Emily thought he was Tom—snagged the spot beside Will so he could discuss the different 401k options that his company was offering to its employees.

If the Daileys were a solar system, it was obvious that Will was their sun. She supposed that was the prerogative of the oldest in a large family. After their parents, it would be natural that the siblings would look to their big brother. If Mr. and Mrs. Dailey had been in attendance at the party, she assumed they'd be the ones dandling the little ones on their knees after the dinner was over. But with the absence of grandparents—had they retired to another state or were they away on a trip?—it was left to Will to hold the baby while admiring a tiny ballerina's uneven pirouettes and toddler Todd's shiny dump truck.

Still, he caught Emily's hand on her last pass to help clear the table. "I'm sorry. Are you doing okay?"

"Fine." Looking at him with a baby slumbering on his shoulder, she felt herself go woozy. Who could blame her? It had to be hardwired into thirty-something women. The urge for the man, the marriage, the baby.

But Will wasn't hers. Not really.

Right?

Yet Will was gazing into her eyes, and maybe he looked a little dizzy, too, like those possibilities that had showed up on the Vegas dance floors were once again whispering in his ear.

One of his hands found hers. "Emily…" His thumb brushed across her knuckles and a rush of goose bumps sped up her arm and across her chest. She clapped her free arm over it so he wouldn't see the instant reaction of her nipples. But maybe he noticed anyway, because his eyes seemed to darken. "*Emily…*"

"Will! Will!" They started—both of them, and the baby, too—as Betsy's voice called from inside the house. "Come into the family room. You haven't seen the video of my graduation."

Instead of being reluctant like the first time his sister had demanded his attention, this time Will hastened away. Emily followed more slowly, and found a place on the outside of the small group huddled around the big-screen TV.

"Whoops, rewound too far," Betsy said, the remote in her hands. "This is stuff from Jamie and Ty's wedding."

On the screen, Will was walking his sister down the aisle.

Will was walking his sister down the aisle?

The screen fuzzed out, and then it changed to show the moving image of Betsy, in a gleaming white cap and gown, her smile even brighter as she ran toward the gathered family and went straight for...Will.

Her first boisterous hug went for brother Will, who was grinning as he pushed her away so he could hand over a huge bouquet of flowers. Where were Mr. and Mrs. Dailey? She'd met them a couple of times when they'd picked up Will at camp, and she couldn't imagine why they weren't in the video footage.

Her confusion must have shown on her face, because Ty nudged her with his elbow. "I heard from Jamie that you and Will were old friends—"

"Summer friends. Until we were seventeen."

"Then I wonder if you know what happened when he was eighteen."

She glanced up. "What? What happened?"

His voice lowered. "Their parents died. After that, Will raised them all. Alone. For all intents and purposes, he's been a parent for the last thirteen years."

A parent for the last thirteen years.

Oh. Oh, Will. Her throat tightened. "Until Betsy graduated."

"Yep. He was in Vegas last week—the first real vacation he's ever had. He's been waiting all this time to finally become a bachelor."

The words sank in slowly, settling like rocks into the muddy bottom of a stream. Well, she'd wanted to know more about him, hadn't she?

Chapter Three

Emily decided she had to get away. She needed some peace, some time, some distance to process what she'd just learned.

He's been waiting all this time to finally become a bachelor.

She backed away without any of those gathered around the TV noticing, and only turned as she heard clattering from the kitchen. With a quick movement, she ducked around the corner to find Jamie putting away leftovers.

"I wanted to say thank you," Emily said, sketching a wave. "I should probably be heading home."

"We're going to have dancing. And I haven't set out dessert yet," Jamie protested. "Your cake looks delicious."

"I hope you enjoy it. But I…I have an early day at the library tomorrow."

The other woman made a face. "We scared you away."

"No!" Will's family hadn't scared her. "You're all very nice."

"We're loud."

"But in a nice way." Emily smiled. "Really. But I do have work tomorrow."

A child's cry warbled into the room, and Jamie cast a glance at the baby monitor on the counter. "Uh-oh. Polly wasn't quite ready to go down."

"You check on her and I'll let myself out," Emily said. "Thanks again."

After another hug, Jamie disappeared and Emily had her chance to make a getaway. When she saw that Will was still absorbed in the video, she decided to make it a silent, unannounced retreat by letting herself out through the side gate in the backyard.

The dancing had already started on the large deck. Dusk was descending, and the railing was strung with lights in the shape of hula dancers. As she passed one of the other women—Chelsea? Ann?— the small dancing partner that was propped on her hip held out his chubby arms to Emily.

"You now," little Todd said.

She halted. "What?"

He repeated the words, his body angling toward Emily. "You now."

Her eyes met those of his spurned partner. The other woman grinned. "He likes to spread his love around. What can I say? That's a guy for you, isn't it?"

And what could Emily do but take hold of the toddler? As she swayed to the slow beat of a country song, the boy's smile could have melted steel. She shook her head. "Did your Uncle Will teach you your way with women?"

But before he could answer, his Uncle Will was there, lifting his nephew away from her to set him on his feet. "Your mom's looking for you."

The boy scowled. "Unc—"

Will held up a hand, halting further protest. "Cake." Short legs churned in their hurry to get to the kitchen.

Emily had to laugh. "You're good at that."

"Practice."

She nodded. "Right." And that reminded her she'd been on her way out because the bachelor before her had earned his freedom. She took a step back.

"You wouldn't happen to be running away from me again, would you?"

"Of course not," she lied, even as she edged back some more.

"You sure about that?" He pulled her into his arms

as the song coming through the speakers slid into Bonnie Raitt's "I Can't Make You Love Me." Will gathered Emily nearer as Raitt's bluesy voice petitioned a man to just hold her close.

Emily's eyes shut as Will's big hands led her into moving with the beat of the slow and sultry song. It was Las Vegas all over again, the smell of his skin, the beat of his heart against hers, the notion that it was Will, her Will, who was holding her that pushed away all other concerns.

His hand moved up to tangle in her hair, and she nestled closer, tucking her cheek in the cup created where his shoulder met his chest. He felt so solid. So strong. Like he could hold up the weight of the world.

The weight of a family. He'd been doing that for the past thirteen years.

He's been waiting all this time to finally become a bachelor.

And yet she was hanging on to him as if he belonged to her. Forcing herself to move back a few inches, she looked up at him. "Will, you never told me about your parents. I'm so sorry."

His movement hitched a moment, and then he returned to that soothing, back-and-forth rock. "It took me a long time to believe what happened."

"What *did* happen?"

He gave a shrug. "Car accident. I'd just turned

eighteen. Betsy was eight. Everyone else was in between."

"And they became your responsibility."

That same cool shrug. "Yeah. I'd been planning on college, but after…after the accident, my dad had a friend who could get me on as a firefighter once I made it through the academy after finishing high school. Which I did, a semester early. The hours were long, but it was a way to keep us together. So I went for it, and everyone pitched in."

With Will bearing the brunt of the duties and the worry, she guessed. "You should have written me. Called."

He was already shaking his head. "What were you going to do, Em? You were hundreds of miles away and all of what…seventeen?"

"But—"

"I handled it, Emily. I handled it just fine on my own."

She swallowed her next words, though it was on the tip of her tongue to tell him she would have liked to have known, if only to have winged a few good thoughts his way. But he, apparently, hadn't wanted anything from her then.

He was right, she supposed. She'd been a teenager, and they'd been… What had they really been to each other then? Teenage crush? Summer fling?

Still, her heart ached a little that he hadn't turned

to her all those years ago. Ignoring the hurt, she pasted on a smile. "Well, in any case, it looks like you did a great job. They're nice people, Will, your brothers and sisters. Everyone here."

"Including my competition, right?"

"Your competition?" She hadn't noticed another man that night besides Will. "What are you talking about? *Who* are you talking about?"

"About two feet tall? Towhead? You've already forgotten the guy in whose arms I caught you not ten minutes ago?"

She laughed. "Oh, yeah. He's nice people, too. Though short. I like them a little taller and a little older than that."

"Really?" He drew out the word as he drew her close again. "Why don't you tell me exactly how you like them."

The fun, flirtatious tone was exactly how he'd played her last week. In Las Vegas, his warm, free and easy manner had completely disarmed her, evaporating her normal caution and innate common sense. It had been so darn attractive and so darn seductive that she'd never imagined there were deeper, colder currents running beneath all that surface charm and smoldering sexuality.

"You should have told me in Las Vegas, Will," she murmured.

"What?"

"You should have told me about your parents, your family, what you've gone through."

His feet stopped moving. Dusk had turned to night, and he'd danced them into the shadows of the eaves. "Why the hell would I tell you any of that?"

"I don't know," she answered, moving back so her shoulder blades bumped the wall of the house. "It's a pretty big thing about a person."

"So you think I should go around spilling my guts to every pretty lady I meet?" There was a trace of irritation in his voice. "You think that I need their pity to get their interest?"

"No." Every pretty lady? How about just the ones he married? "That's not what I said. But when you want to get to know a woman, build a relationship—"

"I'm not interested in 'getting to know' women. I don't want 'relationships.' Not in the way that you mean. Do you realize that when other guys my age were hitting on chicks and heading out to parties that I was at home *giving* parties, and showing little kids how to hit piñatas?" His voice was low, rough. Obviously she'd poked a sore spot.

"Okay, but there'll come a time—"

"Now's the time, Emily. *My* time. I don't need a relationship that will tie me up or tie me down. God, I've been there, done that, and washed all the freakin' T-shirts. And the sheets, and the towels and three-thousand pairs of socks. Do you know how many socks a family of six goes through in a week?"

She might have laughed, if he didn't sound so serious. "Okay, okay. I understand."

He made a disgusted sound and turned away. "You understand nothing." Then he spun back, and yanked her close again. "Or if you do, explain it to me. Because I don't understand *this*."

His mouth slammed into hers.

Her heart jumped, her lips parted, and as his tongue slid into her mouth she rose to her tiptoes to get even closer to him. One of her arms wrapped his neck, one of his scooped around her hips and pulled her against his pelvis.

His body was hot, the part of him pressing against her stomach was hard and insistent and she pushed herself harder against it, wanting friction. Closeness. Wanting Will.

His hand slid up her side and his mouth angled for a tighter fit just as his fingers closed over her breast. The pleasure of it made her gasp, and then that little bit of fresh oxygen reached her brain and made her wake up to where they were.

What they were doing.

Why they shouldn't be doing it. He'd been waiting thirteen years to be a bachelor, to have *his* time, to be heading out to parties and picking up women other than the one who was—just for the moment—his wife.

Making a sound of distress, she broke the kiss. His arms dropped instantly, but Emily ran anyway.

Too late, she worried. She'd run from him too late.

The small house was a beige stucco, cottage-styled, with the door painted a mossy green. Will stared into the grated, hand-sized, eye-level window cut into the wood that served as a peephole. No bright blue eyes stared back, despite the fact that he'd rung the bell, knocked, then rang the bell a second time.

He drummed his fingers on his thigh with frustration. After Jamie and Ty's party, he'd kicked himself for forgetting to get her cell phone number. That had him heading back to the library only to discover that Emily had deserted her post. According to her boss, she'd called in sick. It had taken two days and all the charm at his disposal—not to mention showing up in his firefighter's uniform—for the older lady to give in and give him Emily's address so he could "check up on her."

But she was either ill enough to suffer hearing loss, or she was avoiding him.

Was it the latter? Was there a reason she wouldn't be as eager as he to sever that impulsive knot they'd tied in Las Vegas? He hoped to hell that wasn't the case, because it was his plan to task her with finding out what steps were necessary for them to get a divorce or an annulment or whatever. She was the reference librarian, after all.

And he was a bachelor on a mission, he reminded himself as he once again banged his fist against the door. A bachelor on a mission to live like a single man should. His rash action in Las Vegas had already made him break his vow to keep clear of his family. Now he needed his connection with Emily separated before it caused other unintended consequences.

When his next knock came and went unanswered, he felt an uneasy chill creep down his spine. This was the right address. That was her car in the driveway, he'd bet on it, because the sticker on the back bumper was a plain giveaway: *Reading Is Sexy*.

Grateful he was still in his Paxton FD uniform, he stepped over the low fence that corralled her side yard and made his way around to the stamp-sized back garden. The rear door to the house was open, only the screen across the opening, and when he peered inside what looked to be a narrow den, he saw a figure curled on a loveseat.

"Em?" he called. "Emily?"

The figure twitched, then stilled. He supposed it was Emily, it was Emily-colored hair that was hanging over the place where the body should have a face, so he pulled open the screen and stepped inside.

"Em," he said again. Crouching down beside the loveseat, he palmed the hair away to expose her features. Emily's pale features. So pale, that her brown lashes were a startling contrast to her white cheeks. "Emily."

Her eyes slowly opened. They were a dull version of their usual blue. "Oh. This isn't heaven."

"What? I look like the devil?"

"No." She drifted off again, her words a mumble. "But I was hoping to move on to a better place."

He settled onto the rag rug covering the hardwood, and stroked her hair to rouse her again. "You really are sick, huh?"

Her eyes stayed closed. "Do firefighters like Dalmatians and posing half-naked for charity calendars?"

"*What?*"

"You should, you know. Izzy says…Izzy says you have a great body."

"What?"

Her eyes popped open. She blinked. "I'm not dreaming. You really *are* here."

"Yep."

She stared another moment. Then she closed her eyes again, as if her lashes were too heavy to hold up. "Go away."

"I can't—"

"I'm *sick*."

"And I've been around a dozen or so sufferers of the Firefighters' Flu—what I'd venture a guess you have—in the past couple of days and am so far unscathed. As a matter of fact, it was probably me who exposed you to the virus in the first place."

She looked at him again. "Then I hate you. Go away."

"You know," he said, propping his shoulder against the cushion of the loveseat. "They say men are lousy patients, but in my experience, it was the girls who were the worst. When she didn't feel well, Jamie could make the whole house miserable with her bad temper. Betsy wasn't a complainer, but she'd insist I hold her hand the whole time she was in bed."

"I don't want you to hold my hand in bed."

And if she was in bed—no, no, he wasn't going to go there, not even in his imagination. He cleared his throat. "Look, can I get you anything?"

"No."

His conscience pricked him. "I just can't run off. I promised your boss I'd look in on you."

"But you did look. You can see it isn't pretty. Now please leave me alone."

It was perverse of him, he knew that, but the more she tried to push him away, the more stubborn he got about staying. Until he could do something for her at least.

"How's your stomach?" he asked.

"I might have lost it altogether sometime last night. As a matter of fact, I hope that's the case."

"It's been quiet since then?"

He took her head movement as a yes. "Then you need liquids. Water. Gatorade."

Without waiting for an answer, he found his way to the kitchen. No Gatorade, but she had a low-calorie version of the stuff in a sports bottle and that would do. It was the electrolytes and the liquid that her body thirsted for.

When he got back she didn't protest much as he helped her to a sitting position and brought the bottle to her mouth. She tried to hold it herself, but he brushed her weak hand away and she ended up leaning on him as she took greedy sips.

"Not so fast," he murmured, brushing her hair off her face again. He wondered how many times he'd done something similar for one of his siblings. "Take it slow."

She turned her face away and he lowered the bottle, as she continued to rest against him. A few minutes later they repeated the process. Two more times, and she pronounced herself feeling steady enough to get up and make a trip to the bathroom.

A muted half shriek from the hallway had him dashing the few feet to find her, staring aghast at her reflection. She met his eyes in the mirror over the sink. "I did die, and hell is that you had to see me looking like this." Her hand gestured to the wild state of her messy hair.

He grinned. "You always know a woman's feeling

better when she's worried about her hairstyle or the size of her butt."

"Later, I'm going to be insulted by that," she said, her voice weary. "But right now I don't have the energy."

To hide his second grin, he pulled open the door to the shower stall and adjusted the taps. "Save your strength for some soap and water. You'll be fifty percent better once you get out."

"I'm not settling for less than eighty-five."

"Sixty."

"Eighty."

"Sixty-five."

"Pessimist," she said, as he let himself out into the hallway and shut the door behind him.

Even sick, she made him smile.

He was glad she didn't take long in there. The idea that he might have to barge in and rescue her, naked and wet, wasn't a prospect he was feeling as clinical about as he should. When she pulled open the bathroom door, he was waiting nearby, his back braced against the wall, and they stared at each other a long minute.

Her wet hair was slicked back from her face. He smelled sweet shampoo and minty toothpaste and her pallor was warmed by a flush brought on—he supposed—by the hot shower. The pink color ran from her cheeks and down the flesh of her neck, all the way to the vee of her chest exposed by her tightly wrapped, white terry cloth robe. She moistened her lips with the tip of her tongue. She'd rubbed something on them, because where they'd been chapped before, they were now already shiny.

His glance slid away and he straightened from the wall. "I made some soup I found in your cupboard. And oyster crackers. Where shall I bring it to you?"

"You don't—" she started, stepping forward, but then she wobbled, and had to grab the doorjamb for support.

He leaped to her, wrapping her waist with his arm. "Let's get you to bed."

The shuddering sigh that went through her body was the only answer he needed. In minutes she was tucked between floral printed sheets and he was settling a tray of soup and crackers across her lap.

She murmured a thanks, then looked up. "You have to go now."

"I will, when—"

"I'm not one of your charges. I'm not your responsibility."

Irritation flashed through him. Okay, and maybe a half dose of guilt. "Gee, Em. Your gratefulness overwhelms."

Her mouth set in a stubborn line. "Take offense. And then take it and yourself out of my house."

"I take it back," he said, scowling. "You're more like Jamie than Besty after all."

"It's just that…" Her shoulders slumped. "It's just that after all you've done for others you don't deserve being saddled with another person to care for."

It didn't feel like saddling. It felt like…hell, he didn't know. And she was right. He wasn't responsible for her and damn sure didn't want to be. His footsteps backed toward the door. "Fine, then. But you should call someone."

"I'll ring Izzy."

"Can she come from wherever she is to make sure you're all right?"

Emily shook her head. "I told you I don't need a keeper."

But looking wan and fragile like that, she did need someone, he thought. "I know your folks are at the other end of the state, but can you call them? Maybe your mom could come stay for a few days."

"Oh." A strange expression crossed Emily's face. "No. My mom and dad are gone now."

"What? When?" He thought she'd been close to them as a kid. If he remembered right, they'd had Emily late in life and she'd been an only child.

"My dad had a massive heart attack when I was twenty-five. Then I stayed with my mom in our old house for the next few years. She had a couple of strokes about eight months ago—the last one…well, it was the last one."

"Oh. I'm sorry, Em." She'd said those same words

to him a couple of days ago, and though he realized she was years older than he'd been when he lost his folks, he knew it still had to hurt.

"That's when I decided to make a move," she said. "I needed to get away from all those old memories to make a fresh start in a new place."

Meaning she was away from all that was familiar, he realized. And that meant she was here in his part of the state, in his *county* knowing no one but him. Having no one, but him.

Her husband.

Hell.

Maybe another bachelor could have pushed that out of his mind right now. Maybe another man could have brought up to her—sick or not—that they had to get on that quickie divorce. It was the kind of bachelor he'd always thought he would be someday.

Or not.

Because, God, he couldn't do it. Separating himself from her at this point would leave her all alone. Without him, who would have gone looking for her when she didn't show up at work? As yet, no one knew her well enough—heck, how many people even knew her phone number or new home address?—to make sure she was safe. Not to mention happy.

Will's fingers curled into fists and he shoved his hands in his pockets to hide his frustration. There wouldn't be any quickie divorce or speedy annulment. Not yet. He couldn't break his ties with Emily until he found her a community of friends, a circle of caring people who would let him finally leave her for good—and leave him with a clear conscience.

Chapter Four

Emily was back at her new job and feeling like her old self by the second half of the following week. She hadn't seen or heard from Will since he'd come to her aid that day on her couch. Still, when she picked up the phone with the greeting, "Reference Desk," she immediately recognized the voice on the other end.

"Can the librarian tell me the most popular Friday night activity in the county?" he asked.

"*This* librarian enjoys putting a dent in her to-be-read pile of books," Emily answered, "but if you'll let me put you on hold a moment, Will, I'll research how the rest of the Ponderosa County residents like to celebrate TGIF."

"No, no, no hold," he put in hastily. "I haven't had a minute to spare this week thanks to a second wave of Firefighters' Flu and I'm afraid I might never reach you again. I want to—"

"Talk, I know," Emily interrupted, guilt making her toes curl in her sensible low heels. "I've been meaning to get in touch with you, too."

He'd been right about the Danielle Phillips thing. Emily indeed had the ostrich-like habit of trying to ignore unpleasant or uncomfortable circumstances in the hopes they would go away. But burying her head in the proverbial sand—or in this case, bookshelves—wasn't going to fix what hot Vegas sun and too many mojitos had wrought.

She plucked the pencil she had tucked behind her ear and brought forward a scratch pad. "Obviously I'm the one who has the skills to find out the best way to—"

"I don't have time for that now," Will suddenly said.

Through the phone, Emily heard the clang of an alarm and then other commotion—pounding feet and maybe the clink of equipment?

"We've got a call," he continued, his voice hurried, "so I have to make this quick. Will you go with me to the Paxton High football game tomorrow night?"

"Um…well…" She really *had* planned on spending the following evening reading.

"Listen, Em, I have to hang up. Six o'clock? I'll meet you at your place."

And before she'd managed to do more than stutter, he ended the call.

She stared at the receiver in her hand. That conversation had been too rushed and definitely less-than-satisfying. Sort of like their marriage.

Blood rose on her cheeks at the errant thought. She should be thankful they hadn't consummated their bad decision instead of complaining about it! Still… Closing her eyes, she remembered the sensation of being in his arms on the dance floor in Las Vegas. She recalled the hot, male scent of his neck when she pressed her face there, the imprint of his large hands on her back and then sliding lower, the unmistakable ridge she'd felt pressing against her stomach as they swayed together.

Squeezing the phone tight, she wrenched her thoughts away from the past. And from what wasn't to be.

Instead, she promised herself she'd focus on discovering what needed to be done to put an end to their impulsive mistake. Friday night, she'd present her findings to him first thing.

Okay, "first thing" wasn't going to happen, Emily realized, when she found herself squeezed between Will and his youngest sister on the bench seat of his pickup. Betsy had insisted on giving her the spot closest to her brother.

"Nice to see you again," the other woman said, "though I'm sorry to horn in on your date."

"Oh, we're not…" Emily let her voice trail off. Explaining they were only out together in order to discuss their divorce was surely subject matter Will didn't want her pursuing with his little sister.

And it would have been a lie, anyway, Emily realized, as they made their way into the crowded stands. While Betsy went off in one direction, Will was hailed by a group who scooted down the bleacher seats to make a place for two on a plaid woolen blanket. Thigh-to-thigh and arm-to-arm with him on one side and a total stranger on the other— not to mention knees to shoulder blades with other people she'd never met—meant they wouldn't have a chance to get into anything serious.

The man beside her stuck out his hand. "Patrick Walsh," he said, with a friendly smile. "Let me guess, you met Will at Roady's. Or was it that new bar over on Chestnut?"

Emily blinked. She looked like some woman Will had picked up in a *bar?* she wondered, glancing down at her jeans, boots and wool coat. Okay, the coat was cherry red, and she'd succumbed to some beauty magazine advice about matching her lipstick to the color of the clothes closest to her face, but she hadn't ever been mistaken for a barfly type in her life. "No, I—" She broke off to press her lips together, hoping to rub some of the brightness away. "Um…"

Patrick was looking at her expectantly. "Um?"

"Well, you see, we met a long time ago…"

The man laughed. "I get it. I've had one of those *looong* nights myself. You were pub-hopping and can't quite recall where you first said 'how do you do' to our man Will?"

"No!" Not that there was anything wrong with pub-hopping or bars or anything like that, not really. But Emily lived a much quieter life, if you didn't count those few crazy days in Las Vegas. "I'm a *librarian*."

"Oh." Patrick stilled, then scooted down the bench to put another inch between their limbs.

If she'd said "serial murderer" she didn't think he could look more surprised—or was it alarmed? Emily sighed. A reference to books tended to work on some people that way.

The man gave her an awkward half smile. "It's just that I didn't think Will was in a place where he was interested in women, who, uh, read."

Emily ignored the little flame of annoyance sparking somewhere beneath her red coat. "What 'place' is that, exactly, that Will's in? And what are the occupations of his usual type of female companion?"

"Not going there," Patrick said, lifting his hands

in surrender. "So not going there. It's just that we used to call him 'Wild Will' in the old days, and he's been making noises about reclaiming the title now that Betsy's—"

"Graduated and out of the house," she finished for him. "I know about that." But what she didn't know was this nickname he used to have. The Will of her past had been summer-tan, summer-strong, the best swimmer, the fastest with a canoe, the guy who could actually *use* a compass. He'd evicted eight-legged creatures from the girls' cabins without one teasing guffaw and she was certain he'd never participated in a single, stupid panty raid.

So…Wild Will?

Glancing to her other side, she saw that the man in question was deep in a conversation with someone sitting on the bleacher behind him. "When exactly was he called that?" she asked the red-haired man beside her. "'Wild Will', I mean." And *why?*

"High school," Patrick answered, a nostalgic smile overtaking his face. "Want to play a practical joke on a friend? Will was the go-to guy. Looking for a class prank? He had dozens of schemes to make the administration nuts. One year we kidnapped the graduation caps and gowns and held them for the ransom of a longer lunch period. His idea."

"Oh. Well." That sounded harmless enough and very much like the clever Will she knew from summer camp. He'd been the one who came up with the best comic lines for the end-of-season skits.

"Of course, then there was his success with the ladies," Patrick went on, followed by a sentimental sigh. "The stuff of legends."

"'Stuff of legends'?" Over her shoulder, she cast another swift glance at Will, but he had turned away from her to grab a box of goodies being passed down the row. "I didn't realize."

"Oh, yeah. The head cheerleader—a senior—before he could drive. Next year, it was the hot yearbook editor-in-chief. Then there were the twins he took to junior prom. I heard he kept the codes to a dozen girls' home alarm systems in a little black book."

"Codes?" A dozen girls?

"You know. He wheedled out of them—not that they put up any fight, mind you—those codes so he could sneak into their bedrooms at night."

A dozen girls?

"I had no idea," Emily said, her voice a little faint.

"He was a bad boy, our Wild Will," Patrick confirmed. "Envy of the guys, the goal of the girls."

She was trying to absorb all that when Will leaned close to insert himself into the conversation. "What are you two talking about?" His brows met as his gaze darted between Emily and Patrick. "You're not hitting on her, are you, Pat?"

"No, Will," Patrick protested. "No way."

Will focused on Emily's face. "Then why do you look so...so..." He made a vague gesture. "Upset?"

"I'm not upset." A cannon at the end zone boomed, announcing the beginning of the game, and everyone around her directed their attention to the field, including, thank goodness, Patrick and Will.

She wasn't upset.

But she had plenty of time to try to figure out what she *was,* because she'd never been a big fan of football. Who could follow that little dirt-colored ball? And there wasn't much else to think about besides how dangerously low teenage girls' denim rode when they sat and why they didn't seem to feel the draft down the back gap of their blue jeans.

Will—her Will—had been "bad" September through June? How then, come summer camp, was he the attentive, sweet, good boyfriend that she remembered? Not once had he tried wheedling any code out of her that would give him access to her bed. Though their kisses had been frequent and sometimes a little bit hot, he'd never pushed her for anything physical either.

Because when school started up again he had all the nookie he needed?

She shot him an assessing look, but he was focused on the game. Probably because he'd been such a player at one time himself, she thought. And not just the football kind of player, either.

So which Will had she met in Las Vegas? The sweet summer guy or the bad boy on the make?

Annoyance flaring again, she crossed her arms over her chest and turned slightly on the bleacher to study his handsome profile. Before she divorced, she decided, she certainly wanted to figure out which one she'd married.

Betsy had another ride home, Will was relieved to hear, because that left him alone with Emily for the drive back from the game. Something was wrong and he was determined to get to the bottom of it, so he was taking the back roads to her place to give him more opportunity to figure out what was up with her mood. Sometime after the start of the game she'd gone ultra-quiet and had stayed that way through the fourth quarter. It was no way to make new friends.

And a befriended Emily was his path to freedom.

Reaching over, he turned up the heat because the atmosphere in the truck's cab was decidedly chilly. It was nothing like the ride on the way to the high school stadium, when Emily's perfume had teased his nose and her warmth had been pressed close to him. Now she was cuddling the passenger door, closer to it than she'd even been to him during the game when she'd been sandwiched on the bleacher between him and Pat.

Pat.

He remembered her chatting with the other man

before the start of the first quarter. Damn. Had Pat-the-Rat done or said something to offend her?

"He's harmless," Will ventured, glancing over even though he couldn't see her expression because the back route they were taking was just that dark. "Pat, I mean. Whatever he said, it doesn't mean anything."

"Are you calling him a compulsive liar?"

"No, of course not. I just meant that he wouldn't knowingly cause offense. Did he say something rude to you?"

"No. He didn't say anything rude."

"Okay." Will breathed a little easier. "Good. You just seemed a little, I don't know, subdued tonight."

Get a grip, Dailey, he told himself. Emily had been sick recently and then this evening she'd been plopped in the middle of a group of strangers at a raucous football game. He should have thought of a better way to introduce her to new people.

"I'm probably overreacting, anyway," Emily said.

Overreacting? He cast her another look. Overreacting about what? If Pat hadn't said anything offensive, then he must have done something to insult Emily.

Will's hands squeezed the steering wheel as heat shot up his spine. Damn it! The bleachers had been so jammed they'd been packed in like sardines, giving Pat an opportunity to somehow touch Emily. Will's Emily.

Thinking of another man's hands on her creamy

skin—on even the fabric covering her creamy skin—
made him tighten his choke-hold on the wheel. "I'll
break every one of his fingers. I swear, honey, I'll
make him rue the day—"

"That he told me about your bad boy reputation?"

"What?"

"It was a little disconcerting to discover that the
boy I remembered from those summers spent his
school year sneaking into girls' bedrooms."

"Whoa." Noting a familiar turn-off just ahead, Will
clamped down on taking the conversation further until
he'd steered the truck to the right. A dirt-and-gravel
road took him to a stand of cottonwood trees growing
beside the silvery remains of a disintegrating barn. It
was commonly known as a Lover's Lane type of spot,
not that now seemed the time to tell Emily that.

When he'd braked and shut off the headlights, he
turned to face her. "Now, what's all this about me
sneaking into girls' bedrooms?"

The meager moonlight didn't illuminate Emily's
face, but he'd seen it clearly during the football game.
She'd changed so little over the years—time only
honing the delicate edge of her jawbone. She still had
the same long eyes, feathery brows and that puffy
lower lip that only looked one cross thought away
from a pout. He couldn't tell if it was pushed out now,
but he did detect her shrug.

"Never mind," she said. "I don't have any real reason to be bothered by your little black book."

"Black book?" Will had to laugh. "I don't have any little black book."

"Not even in high school? With the home alarm passcodes of your eager and willing teen harem?"

"Good God," Will said, half-amused and half-bothered. "Is that the kind of tall tale that Pat's spouting these days? Next thing you know I'll have a big blue ox, too."

"No, just a date with a pair of twins to the junior prom."

"Oh."

"Ha!" Emily pivoted on the seat and he could feel the heat of her gaze. "So you did take *two* girls to the dance."

Will rubbed his hand over his mouth to hide his grimace. "Would you believe they're my cousins?"

"No."

"Oh," he said again.

After a moment, she surprised the hell out of him by releasing a little bubble of laughter. "Will, did you really take a pair of twins to the prom?"

"I did it for us, honey."

She laughed again, and swung her leg up onto the bench seat between them. "Go ahead, my friend, pull the other one."

He wrapped his hand around her ankle, even as

she tried to tug free of his grip. "Really. Of course I wanted to go to the big dance, but I figured by taking the Wilson twins that I wasn't going to get into a compromising position or succumb to temptation when it was just a couple of weeks before we'd be together again. Danita and Danica watched each other like hawks eye snakes. Neither one could make a move without the other one ready to pounce on her."

"They sound charming," Emily replied, still trying to reclaim the limb he'd captured.

"Yeah, you're right," Will admitted. "Charm wasn't one of their, uh, charms. Still, I left the dance unkissed—or close enough, anyway. Can you say the same?"

"My high school didn't have a junior prom." Her latest yank broke his hold and she retreated to a prim pose—knees and ankles pressed together, arms folded over her chest.

"You know what I mean, Em." He ran a hand through his hair. "We didn't make promises to each other about what would or wouldn't happen during the school year. I admit I spent time with other girls, as I'm sure you did with other guys."

There was a conspicuous quiet from her side of the cab. "Em?"

"So you *were* a player," she said. "A senior girl before you could drive? The twins, not to mention the yearbook editor?"

"Emily—"

"Oh, forget about it," she waved a hand in his direction and then laughed a little again. "I don't know why I even brought it up. That was years ago. Who cares what you did during the school year…or what I thought you didn't do."

"Well, it wasn't as if you spent every September through June sitting at home and pining—" He broke off as her stiff body language finally sank in. "Oh. Oh, Emily."

She waved her hand again. "Don't flatter yourself. I probably was just looking for an excuse to stay home and read. I was bookish even then. More than half the reason my parents sent me to summer camp was to get my nose out of novels and into a little sunshine."

And in said sunshine her creamy skin turned a pale golden shade. It would bring out a splash of freckles on said nose, too.

She sighed. "What a sappy girl I was."

He narrowed his eyes. "Sappy?"

"Silly. Sentimental. Foolish. While you were out dating cheerleaders and twins, I was sitting at home believing we had something really special."

"We did have something really special."

"Thanks, but I'm all grown up now. It's no big deal to realize that while I was drowning in the sea of teenage love, you were skating across its waters."

"Emily." Will shifted from underneath the steering

wheel to move toward her. "I wasn't skating. I was right there with you, the water dangerously close to going over my head. You don't know how much I thought about you—how much I wanted you."

Though he couldn't read her expression in the darkness, he could feel her disbelief. "You never once seemed…out of control, or even interested in pushing for more," she said.

"Because I was so damn afraid of scaring you off," he answered. "Yeah, apparently I had a little more experience than you when it came to kissing, but emotionally I was in a thousand knots when I was near you."

"Really?" This time he could hear a smile in her voice. "Me, too. You'd touch my hand and my stomach would cramp."

"My heart pounded so hard sometimes that I thought you might see it expanding out of my chest like something from a cartoon." Will rubbed his sternum in sympathy for the lovesick kid he'd been. "And for the record, I regarded my, um, experiments with other girls something I did for us, Em."

"You said that before." Her voice was dry. "Excuse me for having a little trouble swallowing it down."

"Really. Remember when I taught you to French kiss? I didn't just pick that up from the Boy Scout manual, you know. That yearbook editor was one smart cookie and my learning experience with her made *your* learning experience just that much more pleasant."

She made a sound of stifled amusement. "Tell me you didn't actually think that…not then and certainly not now."

But the fact was, he sort of *had* thought that. Fine, maybe that made him sound like an arrogant piece of work, but he'd never forget the first time he'd held Emily's sweet face in the cup of his palms and whispered against her lips, "Open. Open your mouth."

And then, without forethought, he slid down the truck's seat and was doing it again, cradling her jaw in his palms, his long fingers caging the soft warmth of her cheeks. Her lashes fluttered and he felt the butterfly flicker against the pads of his index fingers.

His heart started that slamming pound against his ribs as he leaned closer. Her perfume floated in the air, dizzying him with its sweetness, as his lips touched hers.

"Open." He echoed that old lesson. "Open your mouth."

When she did, warm air puffed out, and then he slid inside, just the smallest distance, just enough so that he could touch the tip of his tongue to hers. Her breath hitched, his stomach knotted, and it was like he was a kid again, eager, afraid, breathless, burning up with heat.

Only with Emily had it ever been like this.

Special, sweet fire.

It engulfed him, taking over his common sense,

his caution, all those promises about his future he'd made to himself.

It was so damn hard to think of that future he could start living when the past was so easily preoccupying him.

Chapter Five

The local home improvement store had everything Emily needed, she supposed, if she actually knew everything that she needed. There were butcher-aproned helpers here and there, but every time she tried to catch one's attention, she lost him or her to a more assertive home-improver. Seemed like Sunday afternoon was a popular time for shopping at the place.

She consulted the do-it-yourself manual she'd checked out of the library and then stood staring at the miles of unfamiliar objects and products stretched before her. There was no need to indulge in self-pity, she told herself. This confusion was probably no more than what the latest HGTV cute carpenter would feel if he suddenly found himself in the aisles of beauty products at a Sephora.

But at least Sephora smelled nice.

Emily craned her neck to see if any of the sales-clerks were now free, her gaze hop-skipping around the other browsers in her row. There were two dusty, work-booted guys who looked like they were here to pick up a missing item for their current construc-tion job. Three couples—husbands and wives she guessed—perusing the shelves shoulder-to-shoulder. And over there was a handsome young dad, his tod-dler son riding his shoulders as he shopped.

It struck her heart with a sudden pang that every-body—even at a place that sold wrenches and win-dows—seemed to have somebody.

The sting behind her eyes sent Emily's gaze back to her borrowed book. She blinked a few times and breathed deep, trying to hold back the unexpected sense of loss. And loneliness.

Left without family and in a place far from all that was familiar, there wasn't a soul who cared whether she made it home today—not to mention about any repair job she might want to make *to* the little cottage house. Pushing the thought away, she pressed the back of her hand against her mouth, and focused on the page in front of her.

Should she get patching compound or spackle? Sheetrock and drywall paper tape?

"Emily?"

The masculine voice and its familiar timbre sent her whirling around. "Will?"

But it wasn't the man who'd kissed her with such tenderness the other night. Just that one kiss, before he'd cleared his throat, slid back to his side of the seat, and then drove her home. Just that one kiss—and ever since, she'd been telling herself to forget about it and the man who'd given it to her.

So she should be glad that it wasn't Will who had called her name, and instead was merely two young men who looked very like him. His brothers. With a smile, she took a stab at their names. "Hi, Max and, um, Alex?"

"Tom," the leaner one said. "I'm Tom, but you're right about Max."

"Sorry." She lifted her book to show them what she'd been reading. "I'm a little preoccupied by the differences between drywall and plaster and the holes in them."

Max—she remembered now that he was the second oldest brother in the Dailey clan—glanced over at the page she had open. "You've got a hole in a wall?"

"Ceiling, actually. The fixture was missing from the dining room when I moved in and I have another to replace it, but once I install it there'll be a gap around the base. I need to fill that in."

The young men exchanged a glance. "You're going to do some electrical work as well?"

Emily ran her finger over the bookmark she'd inserted farther back in the manual. "I think I just have to twist some wires together or something."

"Or something," Tom murmured. "Are you, uh, experienced with this kind of thing?"

"No. But I have the book and a set of pink-handled screwdrivers that my friend Izzy gave me one Christmas."

"And a ladder?" Max asked.

"I was going to stand on the dining room table," Emily admitted. "I'll put a sheet down or something, and if I'm still not tall enough, I can stack a dictionary and a thesaurus at the center and—"

"Why don't you let us help," Max said hastily. "We can get our hands on an actual ladder."

"And we have shiny red toolboxes that are full of tools with manly black handles," Tom added.

Emily laughed. "I think my pink screwdrivers work just the same as your manly black ones."

"But the idea of you perched on reference books on top of your dining room table is making me queasy," Max said. "Plus, Will would never forgive us if something happened to you."

"Oh, Will doesn't care what happens to me," Emily

protested, her face flushing. Will was nothing to her nor she to him…except husband and wife. Which they just hadn't quite gotten around to righting yet. "And I couldn't ask you two to—"

"It's the neighborly thing to do," Tom said. "You're new to town. Just consider us like the welcoming committee or something like that."

How could she turn down such a friendly offer when she'd just been lamenting her lack of friends? "You'll have to let me make you dinner afterward."

The two younger men exchanged another glance. "Deal," they said together.

Then they helped her choose her purchases and followed her home. As she unlocked her front door, a round of second thoughts slowed her movements. On the way over, her inner voice had been presenting reasons it was wrong to take them up on their offer. There'd been the whole feminist argument that she was perfectly capable of attending to the task herself, but she'd squashed that one by remembering the repair she'd accomplished the year before. A woman who had made a major fix to a toilet and then mopped up its overflow didn't need to prove anything to anyone.

If she *wanted* to figure out how to install the fixture and patch the ceiling, then she could install the fixture and patch the ceiling. It just so happened that Max and Tom already had the expertise and the superior tools to do the job. There was nothing shameful in acknowledging that.

Except she felt just the teensiest bit of shame knowing that she'd mostly accepted their help because she wanted the company. Company that reminded her a little too much of Will.

"Guys," she said, glancing at them over her shoulder as they tramped up the walkway behind her. "Really. I'm sure I could handle this and I'm also sure you have more important or at least more interesting ways to spend the last of your Sunday."

Max shook his head. "Will…"

That was the biggest problem of all. If he discovered that his brothers had been over doing her home repairs, he might think she was trying very hard to insert herself into his family. To bind herself tighter to him. Yes, they hadn't rushed into dissolving the marriage as quickly as they'd rushed into the wedding itself, but she knew Wild Will wasn't looking for anything the least bit permanent.

"I wouldn't want Will to find out about any of this," she said. "Even that you offered to do something so nice for me."

Her gaze caught on a truck that was rumbling down her street. A suspiciously familiar-looking truck. With a familiar-looking piece of equipment in the back, a red rag tied to the few rungs that were hanging out the back end of the bed.

"That's Will now," she said, looking over at the two young men.

His brothers shared a guilty look, then Tom shrugged. "His was the ladder we could get our hands on. I called him on my cell during the drive here."

"Oh, great." Heat rushed over Emily's cheeks. How mortifying would it be if Will thought she'd connived to get him close again? She'd been doing a pretty good job putting him out of her mind and now this! "I don't want him to think it was my idea to drag him over here."

"We made sure he understood we had to twist your arm," Max said. "And we even offered to go and pick up the ladder. It was his idea to come over and help."

Emily bit her bottom lip and couldn't stop herself from finger combing her hair as she watched him pull up to the curb. "Are you sure?"

"Sure—though I'll be honest and say we didn't exactly try to talk him out of it."

Tom shot a quick glance over his shoulder. "And to be really honest, we were glad to have a reason to get him over here. He's been avoiding the family since June, with only the occasional sighting and we've all been racking our brains for excuses to see him."

Hmm. So maybe that explained why Betsy needed a ride to the football game the other night. "Why don't you just call him up and ask him to go out for a beer or get some dinner?"

"Tried that," Max said. "He says no."

She wasn't sure quite how to put it, so she just threw out her question. "Is it so bad that he wants to leave a little distance between himself and all of you?"

Identical astonished expressions overtook the brothers' faces. "Distance? Why would he want to do that? We're family."

Emily sighed. Will had felt stifled by all the responsibility he'd shouldered, she understood that, but clearly Max and Tom didn't.

"So we'll be owing you, Emily, for this opportunity to hang with our bro."

And how sweet was that? Surrendering to the inevitable, she pushed the front door and held it open for the two guys to walk through. Instead of following them in, she stayed where she was and waited as Will came up her short front walk, toting the ladder under his arm.

"Hi," she said, as their eyes met. Pretending she had a steel rod for a spine and another couple in her knees, she ignored the memory of his calloused hands around her face and the sweet hot touch of his tongue against hers. She cleared her throat and broke their gazes. "Your brothers are already inside."

He paused as he passed her. When she took a breath, she smelled his clean manly scent and stared at the steady beat of his pulse at the notch of his strong neck. "Hi, back," he said. "I hope my brothers haven't been any trouble for you."

"Of course not." She smiled. "They're very nice."

Will was lucky to have them. And as she took another breath of his delicious smell and felt the warmth of his body brush hers as he continued inside, she thought that for a woman who was supposed to be forgetting about him and his kiss, she was feeling pretty darn lucky herself.

It was not that Will couldn't trust his brothers with his ladder. It was not that Will couldn't trust his brothers with his wife—they didn't even know he was married. It was not that Will couldn't trust his brothers to eat their share of a home-cooked meal by a woman who looked like Emily and then follow it up with some proper appreciation.

It was all three together: the ladder, his wife, the spaghetti and meatballs that smelled sinfully good.

"You didn't know I was cooking spaghetti and meatballs," Emily pointed out when he tried to explain why he'd broken away from his important appointment with his couch and televised football to come over and help with the project. "You don't even know whether I can cook or not."

"But my instincts were right, weren't they? It smells great."

"Onions and garlic always smell great." Emily

stirred her sauce again. "Nobody can screw up sautéing onions and garlic."

"I don't know about that," Will answered. "Because I've never sautéed in my life."

"Yes, you did. KP at camp. Sautéing is when we had to stir cut-up vegetables in hot oil."

"Well, I'm certainly out of practice. After that last summer at camp, my veggie prep consisted of ripping open a warehouse store-sized bag of raw baby carrots and tossing it onto the middle of the dining room table. I told the kids we couldn't afford eyeglasses so they better eat up." He had to smile a little, remembering their dutiful crunching.

Emily stood with the wooden spoon in her hand, studying him. "It sounds as if you were a very conscientious provider."

He felt his smile die. "I did what I had to do." It had been a hell of a weight at times, and he thought whole months had gone by when he didn't sleep. "But that's all over now."

Will was getting his easy, breezy bachelorhood back.

Except here he was, in a kitchen that looked and smelled as cozy and domestic as all get out, with his *wife*.

Hell. Without another word, he strode out of the kitchen and then across the hall to the dining room where Max and Tom were putting the finishing touches on the patch job on Emily's ceiling. The new light fixture was already up—a bright, homey chandelier that lit up the small room with its walls painted a soft golden color.

He watched with a little spurt of pride and approval as Tom steadied the ladder as Max climbed down. He'd taught them to be cautious like that, just as their father had taught *him*. They'd done a good repair, too, and cleaned up as they went along, another maxim that Dan Dailey had passed along to his oldest son. Clearing his throat, Will shoved his hands in his pockets. "Looks good. If you're through with the ladder, I'll take it back to my truck."

Maybe, he thought, maybe he should load the ladder, then load himself and head on home. The delicious smells in the kitchen, the camaraderie he'd felt working with his brothers, not to mention the *woman* in the kitchen—he didn't want to get used to any of them, right? A carefree guy like himself could head out to a local watering hole for a beer or two on a Sunday night if he wanted. It wasn't like the old days when he'd be shoving laundry in the gaping maws of the jumbo washing machine and dryer all night, sweating to get the siblings' clothes clean in preparation for another school week.

"Since you guys have taken care of this so quickly, I really don't need to stick around, do I?" he said. And he didn't want to stick around, did he?

Max shot him a grin. "Not on my account. And it wouldn't make me cry if you took Tom with you."

"Tom isn't getting out of your way, Max, without getting some spaghetti and meatballs first," Tom said.

"Getting out of Max's way?" Will echoed. "Huh?"

"And you say you're ready to experience a bachelor's life," Max scoffed. "*Think,* bro. Why would a bachelor be happy to get a beautiful woman alone?"

"Huh?" Will said again, blinking.

"I think she has a very kissable mouth," Max mused, lowering his voice. "Don't you think she has a very kissable mouth, Tom?"

"One-hundred percent very kissable," the youngest Dailey brother acknowledged. "No doubt about it."

"Who?" asked Will, knowing as he said it he was taking the bait. But surely his brothers couldn't mean who he thought they meant. He'd told them he knew Emily from summer camp. But he'd also told them that he and Em were just friends. Still, he didn't believe… "Who's so damn kissable?"

"Very kissable," Max corrected. "I'm talking about our hostess, of course. Tom, I'll give you five bucks to get lost. You won't even have to walk home, because Will here will drive you."

"Five bucks?" Tom heaved in a dramatic breath of air. "And leave the smell of *that* behind? I don't think so."

"Five bucks and when you get back to our place you can have that pizza I've been saving in the freezer."

"Twenty bucks, the pizza and that tube of cookie dough. You promise that, then I'll think about it."

Will looked from brother to brother. "You're talking about Emily? My—I mean, that Emily?" He jerked his thumb toward the kitchen as he glared at the younger men. "Nobody in this house is kissing that Emily, not even for forty bucks, two pizzas and half-a-dozen tubes of cookie dough."

Max lifted a brow, a glint of amusement in his eyes. "Not even you?"

Scowling, Will ignored that. "Just finish up so we can get on with this meal and then get out of here. The three of us together."

But the meal went forward at a leisurely pace, mostly due to Emily. She'd set the table they moved back under the new chandelier with two fat cream-colored candles. They didn't smell at all, Will was happy to note—there was nothing he disliked more than the stench of scented candles. Their flickering light did encourage a man to take a few seconds to chew his food before shoveling in another delicious bite.

And there was Emily's attention to his brothers, too. Though Will hoped to God Max didn't take her polite questions to mean she was returning his interest. He made sure to send his brother meaningful looks that he hoped told the younger man so. Emily was expressing mere curiosity about their lives because she was one of those people who could set a pretty table, serve up good food and also keep dinner conversation going.

All the while causing him to stare at her kissable mouth.

The entire time she had Max and Tom talking about their jobs, the apartment they shared, their broom hockey rec league, Will found himself relaxing in his chair and watching her lips move.

They were a color somewhere between raspberry and cotton candy and while he'd raised sisters and so knew it was likely some lip gloss that helped make them look so tasty, it didn't detract for an instant from their attraction. Or his desire to do that very thing—taste them.

He pushed his plate away from the edge of the table and stretched his legs out, avoiding his brothers' equally long limbs with the ease of long practice. They were laughing about something with Emily now, and the candlelight was shining in her eyes and shining against the very center of her lower lip where she must have just licked it.

He thought of licking there, too, but at the moment was just content to think about it, basking in the warmth of good, hot food in his belly and in the easy company of his brothers. Emily was teasing them about girlfriends now, and Max was trying put some moves on her, but she was laughing that off as well, taking it as the teasing that Will expected it really was, especially after the way his brother shot him a look to see how he took the mild flirtation.

He sent his brother a silent Dailey message, just in case. *Not for you, my friend.*

Max grinned and gave a little nod of acknowledgment, then turned back to their hostess. "And what about you, Emily?"

"What about me?"

"We heard all about your decision to leave Southern California for our northern climes. About how you were looking for a new start after losing your mother last year. But what we don't know about are the broken hearts you left behind…"

She shifted in her seat and then rose. "You're not really interested in that," she said, gathering up the plates. "I'll just—"

"Let the three of us do the dishes," Will said, rising as well, and noting with satisfaction that his brothers did the same. While it had rarely seemed so at home, it looked as if they showed good manners when they were out in the world.

"You've already done enough," Emily protested. "And I'm going to serve brownies next. I can—"

"Sit at the breakfast bar while we clean up," Will said, and headed into the kitchen.

Of course, that went quickly, too. He and his brothers were experts in dishwashing and fell into a natural rhythm.

Emily seemed to appreciate the way they worked. She suggested, anyway, that they hire out at Thanksgiving.

"We're too busy," Tom said. "We make snowflakes on Thanksgiving night."

"Snowflakes?" She looked from one brother's face to another.

Will swallowed his silent groan. Not that the snowflakes were any big secret, but it sounded kind of tacky. Face it, the snowflakes *looked* kind of tacky, but at that first Thanksgiving without his folks, when usually they'd have been unloading from the attic all the Christmas decorations—Daileys had always started the holiday early—he'd come up with the snowflake idea instead, and it had kind of stuck.

"We drag out all kinds of paper and scissors," Tom started.

And did anyone think how hard it was to find six pairs of working scissors in a household of six siblings? Will thought, as he continued to put dishes away. They went MIA like single socks in the dryer.

"And then we sit around after the Thanksgiving meal and cut snowflakes that we use to decorate the house and the tree for Christmas."

"How charming," Emily exclaimed. "How long does that tradition go back?"

As far back as Will's inability to face the attic and all the memories stored there after his parents had died. As far back as Will's grief over his parents' death and his harrowing worry that he couldn't do the job to raise his brothers and sisters right. As far back as the days when he picked up every extra shift at the station to afford to make Christmas a time of cele-bration and gift-giving and not a time of agonizing over where the gifts would come from.

The season had been just another heavy stone around his neck and every day he'd wondered if this was the day he'd drown. He'd loved them all—he was the oldest, he had to, didn't he?—but he was so damn glad to now be free of all that care.

But hell, here in this room with his brothers and his wife…he wasn't free.

He tossed the dishrag he was squeezing onto the counter. "I've got to go," he said, without looking at Max, or Tom, or Emily. "I've got things to do."

Things like getting on with that *vida loca* he'd been dreaming of for the past thirteen years, before he tangled himself up too tightly again with his rel-atives—and his wife—and this time drowned for sure.

Chapter Six

A small tin of the brownies in hand, Emily hurried up Will's front walk, conscious of the passing minutes. She was using the last half of her lunch hour to leave her little token of gratitude. At the bottom of the porch steps, she paused a moment and tilted back her head to take in the farmhouse-styled Dailey family home. The siding was a pearly blue-gray, the trim white, the porch itself wide. It was a charming residence, with a vintage-looking swing placed at the left of the front door. For a family of six kids it wasn't a large place, though, and she could imagine the rough-and-tumble chaos that must have existed within its walls during their growing-up years.

To her, the idea of constant company and ever-present noise sounded more than appealing, but it was obvious that Will had had his fill of it. Now he was in a place where solitude and independence were his dearest wish. She didn't think she was wrong in deducing that he'd left dinner early the night before because he'd felt a need to be alone.

And he'd left so quickly she hadn't been able to properly thank him. But when he came home to find baked goods on his doorstep she hoped he'd get the message she hadn't been able to deliver in person the night before.

She stood on the porch, contemplating the best place to leave her tin, when the front door suddenly opened. Surprised, she stepped back, and Will did, too, so that she couldn't read his expression as he stood in the shadowed foyer.

Besides startled, how did he feel about seeing her again? Annoyed? Glad?

Because glad was how she was feeling, darn it all. Every time, since bumping into him on that hotel pathway in Las Vegas, she'd experienced the incredible, giddy gladness at the sight of his dark hair and handsome features.

"Emily," he murmured now. "I didn't expect to see you."

"I didn't expect to see you either," she said, using her free hand to smooth the skirt of her knee-length, crisp cotton shirtdress. Though it was sunny and warm outside, she wore sheer thigh-high stockings over her bare legs as defense against the air-conditioned cool of the library. "I thought you'd be at work."

"I'm off today," he said, gesturing toward the interior of the house. "Come on in."

"Oh, I…" Surely it was good manners that accounted for his polite words, and not a true welcome. So she should shove the brownies at him and then hit the road herself—she was on the waning half of her lunch hour after all. Really, she should go. But she was as curious as the next temporary wife to see how her temporary husband lived, and she supposed she'd never have another chance. "I can only stay a minute."

Inside, he led her to a narrow living room that was filled with a paisley, overstuffed sofa and a striped loveseat in similar muted colors. Framed artwork, bright and charming but obviously child-rendered, adorned the walls.

Will noticed the direction of her gaze. "A few years ago, the sibs each gave me their best piece of school art for Christmas."

Even at a "few" Christmases ago, some of the paintings had to hark back to elementary school. "You had saved all their art?"

Will shoved his hands in his pockets and shifted

on his feet. "I've got a file for each one of them. My mom started it."

And he'd continued the practice. It shouldn't melt her heart like it did, but the fact was, there now was a warm liquid center in that organ beating in the middle of her chest. Rubbing her knuckles against her breastbone, she crossed to a small upholstered chair to examine a loosely and unevenly stitched afghan in shades of olive green and eggplant yarn, an extraordinarily unattractive combination that clashed with every other color in the room. Certainly another handmade item. She cocked an eyebrow Will's way.

He shifted on his feet again and cleared his throat. "Betsy made that in high school for me. Even she admits now that it's butt-ugly. I've been meaning to get rid of it."

Emily's heart went softer still as she hid her smile. Call her crazy, but she'd bet that Will would be proudly displaying the thing when he was ninety years old. "I like it," she said. Then she noticed the time on the grandfather clock that stood in a corner of the room. While she thought she could spend the rest of the afternoon exploring Will's environs and figuring out what they said about the man he had become, work was waiting for her. "I should be getting back."

"You haven't said why you came by in the first place."

She lifted the tin of brownies. "I wanted to leave

a little thank-you for your help yesterday. Brownies. I realized that you missed out on dessert last night."

"I regretted that." He looked down at his feet, clad in a pair of well-used running shoes.

With his hair damp at the ends, and in a worn pair of jeans and an untucked, rumpled dress shirt that he'd rolled up at the sleeves, he looked like a man about to embark on a few errands. But for all Emily knew, he had been heading out to meet a hot date…or had just tumbled out of bed after a long, late night with one.

She frowned at his bent head, a little mad at him now, and almost wishing she hadn't brought him brownies after all. Let the woman—women?—Wild Will was dating give him the goodies.

Which they probably were, she thought with an internal grumble. Yes, okay, it was stupid to feel betrayed, but she knew she was frowning more fiercely at him anyway.

He caught her wearing that expression, because he suddenly looked up and said, "I regretted even more missing out on learning about the loves you left behind."

Her slack jaw neutralized her previous disapproving expression. "What? What are you talking about?"

"Your romantic past. It struck me sometime after I came home last night that you very neatly side-stepped Max's question. The one about the broken hearts you left back home."

She set the tin of brownies onto a side table, taking her time to line up the little box. "Here is home now."

"Nice try, friend."

She shot him a look. The fact was, they weren't even friends, were they? Old acquaintances, two people caught up in a mutual, whimsical mistake— that they really should do something about, like *now*, but she hated to be the one to remind footloose and fancy-free Wild Will that he was still actually, legally, married. Just because of that she had no obligation to explain to him that she'd spent her twenties as the embarrassing cliché of a librarian who spent most of her time nose-to-book instead of lip-to-lip with some man.

There was no reason to give any of that away.

"Look," she said, making a big play of checking her watch. "I'm busy. I need to get back to the library."

Will's eyes narrowed, and then a grin broke over her face. "Ha. I get it now."

She crossed her arms over her chest. "Get what?"

"That little phrase came too easy for you, sweetheart." He shook his head. "'I'm busy. I need to get back to the library.' Has that been your standard line for the last thirteen years?"

No. While earning her degrees it had been, *I'm busy. I need to study at the library.*

So sue her, she hadn't been much of a party girl or an amateur man-hunter. It wasn't because she'd already given her heart away. Nothing like that. During the years since she'd last seen Will, there'd been other things to do besides finding the man of her dreams.

"I spent a lot of time with my mom after my dad died," she heard herself say. Looking down, she toyed with the brownie tin. "And she needed a lot of care the last couple of years. So I did that when I wasn't working."

"Oh, hell." Regret edged Will's voice as he strode across the space separating them in order to smooth his hand over her hair. "I'm a jerk for teasing you like that, Em. And for reminding you of unpleasant things. I'm sorry."

"It's okay." She shouldn't like the way he stroked her again with his hand.

"No, it's not. Go ahead and hit me or something."

With a little smile, she looked up. "Will…"

Whatever she was going to say got lost in the short distance between them. Her smile faded away as she stared into his eyes, their deep brown color so familiar, the heat in them so distracting.

Exciting.

Memories flooded her, but not those childhood summer memories that had been so sweet when she'd first recognized him in Las Vegas. These were adult memories—the heat of his chest through his shirt as they danced on the hotel bar's tiny parquet floor. The crazy beat of her heart as they said their marriage vows in front of a lousy Elvis impersonator to the strains of "Are You Lonesome Tonight." The way she'd fallen into the deep kiss he'd given her at his sister's barbecue. The quake to her system when he'd touched his tongue to hers in his truck the night of the football game.

Will's fingers curled into her hair, taking hold of it so he could tilt her head back and get a clearer view of her face.

Or a more direct route to her lips.

He let out a soft groan. "Still a boy's dream," he murmured. "Your wide eyes, your soft mouth." His gaze flicked down to Emily's throat. "Why is your heart beating so fast, baby?"

"Because…" She licked her lips, unable to speak more, unable to think. Her heartbeat sped up even more. "I've got to get back. I've got to—"

"Don't go. Don't go anywhere." His free hand moved to her face and his thumb drifted over her cheekbone, and then brushed across her mouth.

Your soft mouth.

The touch to her lips, the remembered words, speared through her. Her body jolted in reaction, her foot taking a quick, unsteady step that had her crashing against the end table. Will released her hair to grab her elbows, just as she felt the unmistakable tug of the nylon covering her calf catching on the leg of the little table.

"Damn," she muttered, and she bent down to inspect the damage. Yep. The run was ugly and climbing higher as she disengaged the stocking's mesh from the rough imperfection in the surface of the wood. Biting her lip, she quickly reached under her skirt to catch the lacy top of the damaged thigh high to draw it off.

At the sound of another low groan, Emily froze. Her gaze lifted to Will's face. The hemline of her dress was nowhere near immodest—it had only risen an inch or two as she sought the top of the stocking— but from his expression she might as well have been performing a striptease in one of the clubs they'd walked past on the Las Vegas Strip.

She might have left the thigh high as is, but it was already pooling at her ankle, so she quickly stepped out of it, then slid her foot back into her low pump. "I…it was an ugly run…"

"Nothing is ugly when it comes to you, Emily."

Oh, wow. Every word, every moment with him, was just melting her more. "I've really got to go," she said again, reminding herself.

"Okay," he answered, but he sank to his haunches in front of her. She swallowed, hard, and then harder as his hand touched the knee of her other leg. "But we can't have you going out unmatched."

And then, she couldn't believe it, then he reached up under her dress, his fingertips sliding upward, over her stocking and then to the lacy top piece until he encountered bare skin. Goose bumps broke out from that point and rushed toward her heels and toward her—well, upward.

Still, she couldn't move.

Frozen by the intimacy of the act, by the eroticism of it, she could only watch as he peeled the nylon from her leg, baring it like the other. When it came time, she put her hand on his shoulder to balance herself as she stepped out of the stocking and stepped back into her shoe.

Will slowly rose, the thigh-high balled in his hand. She reached for it, but he shook his head, then shoved the mesh in the front pocket of his jeans. "You'll get it back tonight, Em."

"Tonight?"

He smiled, and skated his thumb across her bottom lip. "You'll come back for it, won't you?"

You'll come back for it, won't you?

The question plagued her all afternoon. She knew what would happen if she returned to Will's house. The certainty of that had been in the crackle of the air between them in his living room and in the sensitivity of her skin to his slightest touch. But it was a terrible idea to act on that…wasn't it?

But…

Maybe if they did go through with it, if they actually went to bed together, then the distracting attraction would be finally put to rest.

Yeah, right.

Nobody fooled themselves with that argument, did they? If what came after the kisses was as explosive and powerful as the kisses themselves, then she couldn't see how tumbling into Will's bed would smother the fire that always smoldered when they were together.

And if sex between them wasn't any good—

Oh. Might that happen? Could the two of them, skin-to-skin, be more ash than flame?

That potential disappointment sealed the deal, she decided. No way was she getting naked with Will. Much better to live with unrequited sensual longing than the destruction of the sweet memory of their first love if they killed it with a dud of a real sexual experience.

So, yeah, she was going back to Will's this evening, but armed with all the information they needed to start the proceedings to end their marriage, not begin an affair.

Surely, she could withstand even his most experienced attempts to convince her otherwise.

Despite her resolve, though, she was nervous as she got out of her car in front of Will's house. There was still plenty of daylight left and the evening was warm, so it wasn't a surprise to find the front door open—but the sound of country music blasting though the screen was a bit unexpected.

Who would have thought Will was a Carrie Underwood fan? And maybe she was mistaken about the intent of his invitation to return after all, because "Before He Cheats" wasn't a song of seduction.

And then, when she rang the bell, it was his sister, Betsy, who came to the door. She smiled at Emily. "Will said you might be coming by, though he's not here at the moment. I'm turning into your official greeter, I guess, and, I suppose, your official horn-inner of dates with my brother."

Emily felt more relief than you'd expect for a woman strong in her resolve not to go to bed with a man. But with Betsy here, her backbone—or lack thereof— was moot. "I'm not dating your brother," she clarified. "I'm here to, uh…" What excuse could she offer?

Betsy held open the screen door and waved Emily inside. "You're here to help me, if you wouldn't mind. I'm going to one of those come-in-an-old-prom-dress parties and I can always use a second opinion."

"Uh, sure." She followed the other woman down a narrow hallway, then paused at the threshold of a bedroom decorated in a masculine style. "Betsy?"

Will's sister breezed into the room without pause.

"Come on. This room has an extra closet and there's a bunch of old stuff stored in it."

But "this room" was obviously Will's room. And over there, between four posts and under a dark comforter, was Will's bed. And Will's pillow. And the scent of Will in the air.

Across from it was Will's mirror, and beneath it was Will's dresser, and Will's memorabilia was there too—what looked to be photos of his family, and…

Emily's feet stepped into the room without her permission. Because there was another framed photo propped on the gleaming surface. She'd embellished the frame herself, she remembered, finding twigs on her walks with Will and then using hot glue to mount them on the edges surrounding the photo someone had once taken of them. Draped over one edge of the frame was the macramé friendship bracelet she'd knotted for him their last summer together.

She owned a matching one…somewhere.

Okay, fine, she knew exactly where it was. In her jewelry box, tucked between her mother's wedding ring and the heart necklace Will had once given her. Her own wedding ring now rested there as well.

Betsy's voice pulled her out of her reverie. "Emily, which one of these do you like?"

Jerking her gaze off that old photo, she headed toward the younger woman. Inside the spacious, well-lit closet, she found Betsy contemplating a selection of formal dresses that she'd apparently collected off the wooden clothes pole. There were long slinky numbers in jewel tones, a couple of strapless short dresses, another pastel-hued garment with a handkerchief hem, and then a fairytale of a prom dress in a warm coral color with a full tulle skirt dotted with iridescent sequins.

Emily couldn't keep herself away from it. "This one," she said, reaching out a fingertip to touch the puffy skirt. "I always wanted to wear a dress like this."

Betsy made a face. "Can't do it. Brings back terrible memories of Homecoming. I was up for queen. Not only did I lose, but my boyfriend broke up with me that night."

She held a formfitting scarlet satin dress against her. It had a big bow on one shoulder. "What do you think?"

"The bow's a bit…"

"Yeah. Too much. And just right for this party. I'll tell everyone it was Jamie's if I get too much flak for it." She hooked it over the pole and started shedding her clothes. "Though I better make sure I can squeeze into it."

Emily looked over at the fairy dress again. "Are you sure you wouldn't rather wear this one?"

"Ugh, no. I try to think of Denny Jeffries as seldom as possible. Why don't you try it on though? Just for fun."

Emily gazed on it, knowing she shouldn't feel so

wistful. She was thirty years old, much too mature to be drawn to a pretty dress that had teenage fantasy written all over it. But maybe it was because she was in Will's room or because she hadn't attended her own prom or because…well, she didn't know why, but she was suddenly unbuttoning her dress and stepping into the strapless confection.

Betsy had her own garment on and off again—it fit fine, she said, as long as she didn't take any deep breaths—before Emily had the bodice pulled up on the one she was trying on. Zipping up the back required Betsy's assistance, and then she took in her reflection in the mirror mounted on the inside of the closet door.

"Oh." Emily stared at herself. The dress was just as magical off the hanger, and the only thing marring the effect were the parts of her utilitarian bra showing above the sweetheart bodice. "Is it wrong to still believe I was royalty in another life?"

Betsy laughed. "No royal shows her bra straps, though."

"You're right." Sneaking her hand down the front of the dress, she undid the front clasp and drew it out. The bodice had stays in it that kept everything propped up anyway. She turned to the younger woman. "You may call me Princess Emily."

Betsy grinned. "Well, Princess Emily, by your leave, I'm going to have to boogie out of here." She tapped her forefinger against the face of her watch. "I'm late already."

"Okay." Emily returned to admiring her reflection. "I'm just going to pretend for another thirty seconds or so."

Thirty seconds turned into three, four, five minutes. Long enough for Betsy to exit the house and then for Emily to realize she couldn't get the borrowed dress unzipped by herself—meaning that Will might walk in on her any minute wearing something frothy and silly and much too romantic.

It was enough to make her palms sweat as she tried manipulating the recalcitrant zipper again. "Damn, damn, damn," she muttered. Desperate now, she sucked in everything that could be sucked in and managed to spin the dress around on her body so that front was at the back and vice versa.

Of course, that meant her breasts were bared by the low-cut back, but at least she had a shot at getting the zipper to cooperate. With a few swear words spoken as a magic spell, the thing finally released and she drew it down, her air easing out with it. The tulle skirt puddled on the floor at her feet and she was just stepping over the fluffy layers when the closet door swung open.

Her gaze took in Will. Surprise written all over his face, he was staring at her. At her, half-naked.

In his room.

Near his bed.

With the near-audible sound of a match strike, that ever-present spark between them caught, flared to life. Emily's skin flushed and her nipples tightened.

Had she mentioned half-naked? Surely Will hadn't missed it, because his gaze dropped to the tingling evidence of her immediate sexual interest. She threw up an arm to cover her chest.

Another country song was blaring, something about a redneck woman, and it wasn't a seductive musical number either. But it didn't seem to matter, because she'd been seduced already she realized…by the scent of Will in his bedroom, by her photo on Will's dresser, by the serious expression in his eyes as one hand rose and touched the arm that was only doing a so-so job of hiding her breasts.

Chapter Seven

As he half-heard Emily stutter out some explanation about why she was in his closet, Will pulled Emily's forearm away from her body, revealing her creamy breasts and the tight nipples topping them. With his free hand, he reached out to touch one berry-pink point, and he saw it draw to an even smaller bud. Her breath caught, but he didn't look at her face, fascinated as he was by the sight of his big tanned hand close to the delicate colors of her uncovered body.

"A boy's dream," he heard himself say again, as he traced her areola with his forefinger. A blush moved across her chest. "You don't know how long I've thought about this."

"Will…"

He rubbed his thumb over the other peak, and he saw her stomach muscles clench above the elastic band of her pink satiny panties. "I want you, Emily."

He'd been hard for her the first time he'd taken her hand when he was a teenager. At the moment, it felt as if he'd always been hard for her. His gaze flicked up to her face to note her dilated pupils, her parted lips, the expression of uncertainty clearly written there.

"I'm not…I'm not one who is, um, generally swept away."

He smiled a little. Practical Em. Research librarian. It figured she'd want to think everything through. But hadn't they been coming to this since they'd ran into each other in Vegas? He'd thought about it plenty of times since then.

"I'm not trying to turn off your brain, Emily. The opposite in fact." He brushed his thumb over her nipple again and watched the flush rise up her neck to her cheeks. "I don't want to sweep you away. I want you to be right here in this moment, right now, with me."

Her body swayed toward him, then she rocked back on her heels. "But…but…"

"But what?" He drew her forward and slid his hand around her bare back so that his palm was between her shoulder blades and her nipples just a shirt away from his naked chest. "We're too young?" he asked, his voice lowered. "Someone might catch us? We don't want each other?"

She licked her bottom lip, the puffy one that made him crazy just looking at it.

"Emily, you know none of those objections are true. Not anymore for the first two. Never for the third. We're all grown up now. We can touch each other, skin-to-skin, all the good parts for the taking, without worrying about anything."

The face she made was somewhere between a pout, a frown and a smile. "Your arts of persuasion have certainly been honed over the years, Will."

He grinned, rubbing his palm in soothing circles over her spine. "Raising five kids will do that for a guy."

That sent her gaze darting over his shoulder and into the bedroom. "Don't worry, Emily," he assured her. "We're alone. We're going to stay alone. I locked the front door on my way in. It's just you and me and that bed that's never had another woman in it...until you."

Her gaze narrowed. "No. Really?"

With his free hand he rubbed at the little line developing between her brows. "Really." His lips touched hers, soft there too, but he lingered to let their warm breath mingle. "Just another first you'll be for me, sweetheart."

Her heart was racing, he could feel it against his hand and against his chest. It made him want to grab, insist, possess, but instead he stroked his fingers down the speed bumps of her spine, and they reminded him to take it slow. She shivered against him, and he kissed each corner of her lips and then her nose. "Emily, I've wanted to make love to you since before I understood exactly what that meant. You want me too, I know that."

She laid her cheek against his shoulder, snuggling up against him like he was something familiar and comfortable instead of a hard, horny male holding on to his control by a thread. So he held on to it tighter, and held back from grinding against her, from showing how hot he was really running, because this was Emily and he used to spend hours content with merely sifting his fingers through her long, silky hair.

"I'm overthinking this, aren't I, Will?"

"I always said the Honor Roll would get you into trouble, baby."

She laughed. "Believe me. It didn't get me into any kind of trouble at all."

Was that regret he heard in her voice? God, he could empathize. He'd had to go from Wild Will to Responsible Will when he was eighteen years old, and he'd missed being able to indulge in his old rowdy ways. He caught her chin in his hand and lifted it so their eyes met. "Then for once let me be the danger you missed out on, baby. I'll keep you safe."

Her mouth curved. "My danger and my safety—both at once?"

Hell, yeah, he'd be her sinner and her saint, if it would keep that smile on her face and that promise of surrender in her eyes. "Whatever you need, Em."

"Well, then." She took a deep breath in, then let it out.

A decision had been made, he could tell.

"Well, then," she said again, as her hands slid to his chest and found the buttons of his shirt. "What I need, at the moment, is you."

For a woman who used her brain a lot, her fingers were plenty nimble as well. All that page turning, or maybe it was the computer work? Will pondered those for a second or two, just until she was sliding the cotton off his shoulders and bringing her bare skin against his.

He groaned at the goodness of it, his palms sliding down to cup her satin-covered behind. She lifted her mouth to his, and he kissed her, softly again, holding back a moment because this was Emily—finally, Emily! But then he remembered he was her danger and he surged his tongue into her mouth, seeking all her wet, slick surfaces.

She bowed in his arms, her belly pressing against his erection, her perfume rising up to envelop them in a sweet cloud of scented heat. One of his hands speared through her hair to hold her mouth steady for his as his other slid under her panties to palm the globe of her butt.

She made a needy little sound that he swallowed, savoring it like a treat. His prize for making her passion rise.

He tore their mouths apart so he could kiss her soft cheek, the heated column of her neck, the rise of her collarbone. His hands built two shelves for her breasts, and he propped them on his palms, edging back to admire the sight of them.

Held by him.

Held for his mouth.

Bending down, he covered one stiff peak with his lips, appreciating her little gasp of pleasure and rewarding it with the wet greeting of his tongue. Her hands cradled his head and he read the sign. Loved the message.

More.

Harder.

He sucked her flesh deeper into his mouth, holding her hard nipple tight against the roof of his mouth with his tongue to distract her as he eased his fingers over her hips. His thumbs caught in the elastic band of her panties and he switched breasts, playing and sucking as he pushed the scrap of fabric down her sleek thighs.

"Will…" he heard Emily whisper, his name a plea he used to fantasize about hearing on her lips.

It was all so much like a fantasy, like those hot dreams he'd woken up from as a teenager, half-ashamed at how much he wanted his summer girl. But there was no shame in this now, no need for cold showers or thoughts of calculus to smother the need.

Now he could stoke it. He *did* stoke it, by slipping his hand between her thighs and toying with the soft folds of her sex, teasing them open until her liquid arousal spilled over his fingers.

"*Will.*"

It was even easier to play now, with her flesh swollen and slick around his exploring hand. He touched her at the top of her cleft, and she jerked in his arms. He eased up his mouth on her breast, sucking softer, slower, circling her nipple with his tongue in the same rhythm as he circled the bud of her sex with his thumb.

She was pliant, melting against him everywhere, and his erection pulsed against his belly, poker-stiff and ready to find its way to heaven.

But Emily was a thinker, she'd already claimed that, and he wanted to take all her worrisome thoughts away before he took her to bed. He wanted her to accept the dangerous edge he could take her to, and then let him push her over, all the while trusting that he'd be there to catch her as well.

He lifted his head to look at her, almost losing it right then and there. Her eyes were slumberous, her cheeks painted with a passionate pink. Her nipples were wet, reddened by his almost-rough touch, and lower, there was his hand, circling heaven as it delved between her thighs and her tight little brown curls. He could see the glint of moisture on his hand as it moved against her, and the sight was so erotic, so wild, that he had to freeze his movements unless he came right then and embarrassed them both.

But Emily—the librarian, his thinker—wasn't for slowing down or taking pity on what was happening to him. She wrapped her arms around his neck and stepped into his body, squirming in his arms so that her damp nipples rode his pectoral muscles and her soft, hot and petaled sex found what it needed against his fingertips.

Moaning, she pushed harder against him, and he felt more moisture spill over his hand. He followed its path, smoothing one long finger, then two, into the clasping confines of her body, moaning himself now as her interior muscles gripped him and she came.

He watched the release dawn across her face, her lashes falling to her cheekbones, her lips parting on silent, unsteady breaths, her flush racing across her creamy skin to make her even more beautiful.

With anyone else, he would have been hard-pressed to hold off and not move instantly into finding his own pleasure, but then this *was* pleasure, his arms around Emily, his body sheltering hers, keeping her safe as he'd promised, as she came back to herself…and to him.

Shy, he wasn't surprised to discover, as she gave a last little shiver and then glanced up at him from under her eyelashes. But then her hand stroked his chest, heading for a path straight to the fly of his jeans. He caught it, and brought her fingers to his mouth. "I loved that," he said against them. "I loved that and want to do it all over again."

She went on tiptoe to kiss his chin. "Will—"

"Gets to start all over again," he said, his voice firm. And then he walked backward, keeping her warm naked body against his, until the back of his knees hit the bed. He went over, taking her with him.

And then he did it again—went over, taking her with him—with both of them naked and moving together as if they'd been lovers forever…and not just in all his long-ago dreams.

Emily sat across from Will at his kitchen table, her hair damp, her feet bare, her body wrapped in his robe. Resting her chin on her hand and her elbow beside the glass of wine he'd poured her, she watched him move around the kitchen.

He sent her a wry look as he slid a frozen pizza into the oven. "I'm sorry to say it's Italian two nights in a row and nothing as special as the spaghetti you made yesterday. It was our staple Tuesday-and-

Thursday dinners when I was raising the kids and I can't seem to break myself out of the habit of buying and eating them."

Emily waved off his apology, amused by the way that he spoke of his brothers and sisters as "the kids." Okay, he could have called them "the crocodiles" and she would still have been smiling. Sex with Will seemed to put her in a good mood.

She'd had sex before, of course. And she could remember vividly enough how awkward it could be after the first encounter with a man. But this was *Will*. He'd known her before she could fill out a bathing suit. Before she'd started shaving her legs. When she thought the height of devotion was throwing pine cones at the object of her affection.

Will had given her her first kiss and it only made sense that he'd also give her her first stress-free, after-sex experience.

He paused to glance at her again after pulling a bagged salad out of his refrigerator. "You okay? You're quiet, but you look…"

"Fine," she told him, sipping at the red wine and letting it warm her already-warm insides. "I'm just fine."

She spoke the truth. It seemed that the release of the sexual tension simmering between herself and Will had released other tension as well. The last couple of years she'd been in knots, worrying about her mother's failing health and then wondering where she was going in her own life.

Not to mention Izzy's exhortation to get out there and live a little instead of turning to books in order to satisfy her need for emotional experiences. So she'd finally listened, and the result was spectacular...and the aftereffects weren't bad either. There was the residual warmth of sexual pleasure humming through her and the complete lack of need on her part to figure out where she and Will would go next.

She already knew that he wasn't looking for anything serious or long-term, so she didn't have to mine every moment for meaning or intention. She could just sip the wine and sniff the smell of pizza baking and be as happy as she'd be after getting a good haircut and blow-out or a particularly relaxing facial.

Yes. She could look at sex like a pleasant sort of personal grooming experience.

Okay, not that she'd tell Will that, because it wasn't quite right, but the point of view gave her just the perfect attitude as she shared the pizza with Will and then dressed to go home.

He started to make a polite noise about her staying over, but she had to work the next day and so did he. So she walked away without further thought or any future date with him—after all, it wasn't her usual practice to make her next appointment with her stylist upon completion of her current one—and thought Will looked as content for her to go as she was to leave him.

It bugged the hell out of Will that Emily had left him the night before with a carefree salute and an almost-smug smile. That wasn't right, was it?

Not that he'd thought of right or wrong or anything beyond the bed once he'd discovered her half-naked in his closet. Layers of frou-frou dress at her feet, she'd looked like a water nymph rising out of the waves. The only thing he'd been thinking of at that moment was getting her out of her sole piece of clothing—those panties that he had a kinky little hankering to steal from her and then bronze. Not for a second had he put his brain toward what they would do, relationship-wise, after having sex.

But that was a guy-prerogative, wasn't it? To be so taken with the present that he didn't consider the future. But then how was it, when that future came, that Emily was the one strolling away without so much as a "Won't I see you later?"

All right, he realized that wasn't very enlightened of him, and maybe he'd needed to revamp his outlook, but his confusion was less about stereotypical gender roles and more about the woman he'd been with the night before. She had to have been analyzing and cataloging what all this now meant. He knew his heavy-thinking, research-oriented librarian Em.

Didn't he?

Still mulling over what to do about her, during his lunch break at the fire station, he called his sister, Jamie.

"What's happened, Will?" she asked. Her voice sounded alarmed. "What's wrong?"

Will frowned. "Does something have to be wrong for me to call my sister?"

There was a pause. "Well, frankly, yes."

Guilt gave him a little slap. "Everything's just fine," he grumbled. But that word *fine* made him think of Emily again, and of how she'd told him she was fine, too, even though they'd just shared a sexual experience that he found mindblowingly unforgettable.

Yet she'd walked away, without a backward glance, without an acknowledgment of just how… well, damn special they'd been between the sheets. So he'd called his sister to…hell, he couldn't exactly ask her advice about this, could he?

First, he wasn't about to make love and tell. Not to anyone. And second, he didn't turn to the sibs for help. He was the responsible one, the go-to bro, not the one going to *them*. And he really, really wanted to untangle himself from all the familial bonds anyway. He was owed that, wasn't he, after those long years of parent-teacher appointments, butt-numbing sessions on sports bleachers and seemingly endless tuition payments?

"Will?" Jamie said. "Will, if you only called to mystify me, can we postpone it for some other time? I've got cookies in the oven for my book group and the baby's about to throw strained peas at me, and—"

"Strained peas? I'd throw those at you, too," Will said, and considered himself blessed that at least he'd avoided being the caretaker of babies. The kids had been way past diapers and most of them beyond kids meals when he'd taken over. Then another thought struck him. "Did you say something about your book group?"

"They're coming over tomorrow night. It's my turn to host. Why?"

Why not? Will thought. The idea was perfect. He'd get Jamie to invite Emily to her book group the following evening. That way, he could check up on her without being obvious—maybe he'd drop by at the end of the thing—but he'd also provide an opportunity for Emily to make new friends. That was one of his goals, wasn't it? Emily secure in her new community meant he could untether himself from their inconvenient connection.

He still wanted to do that, despite how hot they'd been between the sheets, because, damn it, he was a man determined to enjoy his newly won bachelor status. So getting Emily into his sister's book group was a grand idea.

The more he considered it, the better it became. For several reasons he could think of, not the least of which was that the all-woman book club meeting was a more appropriate avenue for friend-making than that football game. There, she'd run into that boneheaded Pat-the-Rat and Will didn't like what she'd learned from him. At Jamie's female-only event it was highly unlikely that anyone would remind Emily that he was the once and future Wild Will.

Chapter Eight

Emily was still feeling pleased with herself and her world when she went to Jamie's house, taking the other woman up on her last-minute request for Emily to attend her book group night. While the invitation had Will's fingerprints all over it, she'd accepted gladly. No matter how self-satisfied she was over how she'd handled things with him, there was no sense in not giving herself something to think about.

Something besides Will and what they'd done in his bed.

The next day he'd sent her a charming, small bouquet of country flowers. It was a sweet, casual gesture that she took as the message she suspected he intended. They'd had a casual interlude. So it seemed smart to get her mind off Will and onto something else.

Serendipitously—or not, since she was a voracious reader—she'd read the novel the book club members were discussing that night. But it turned out that she was in the minority, since several of the women, many of them young mothers, had been nursing various family members and themselves through the same flu that had flattened Emily. While that larger group commiserated about long waits in the pediatrician's waiting room and the struggles of caring for sick husbands and ailing children when the nurse felt like death-warmed-over herself, a smaller group that included Emily carried on a discussion about the heroine of the book and her travails involving shoe shopping, a married, on-again, off-again boyfriend and the countdown of her biological clock.

"Overextended credit cards, crummy love lives, that annoying tick-tock," one beautiful blonde complained. "I'm tired of single women being portrayed as either on unending quests for the perfect stiletto or sitting through unending evenings with loser guys and sticky cocktails. All because the woman's frantic for something that will in a few years—" she lowered her voice and slid a glance to the group of moms nearby "——be puking its guts out one day and having temper tantrums the next."

"Laurie!" admonished the young woman on the couch beside her.

"What? Haven't you been listening to our friends over there? I'm not seeing the upside to this mommy thing."

Emily hid her grin behind her cup of tea. Laurie's comments were honest and even refreshing and because she didn't look a day over twenty-five, there was plenty of time for her opinion to change. Or not. "I did think that the heroine agreeing to date a guy who worked in the circus showed more desperation than true desire," Emily said.

"Yeah," Laurie added. "Especially when he confessed his job involved a blue wig and a nose that honked when you squeezed it."

Her companion on the couch grimaced. "I once went out with a guy who made balloon animals. But to my credit, he didn't have to dress like a clown while he was on the job."

Laurie clucked. "Still, Gail…"

"It's not easy to meet men! It was that year I worked in the admin office at the all-girls' school."

"What about you?" Laurie asked, turning to Emily. "What's your opinion on motherhood, the dating scene and the best places to meet men?"

"Motherhood, dating, men?" Emily shrugged. "My

opinion is I guess I'd prefer thinking of them in the opposite order. Man, dating, marriage and the rest after that." Her gaze strayed to the nearby mantel where a selection of framed photos was gathered, each picture crowded with Dailey siblings. While she wasn't anxious, exactly, about becoming a wife and mother, family was something she truly missed. An only child, she'd never been part of a large one like the Dailey clan.

She didn't allow her gaze to linger too long on the mantel, though, because she kept staring at the single 8 x 10 of Will. She was supposed to be distracting herself from thoughts of him. "But I work in a library," she said, refocusing on the two women. "It's probably a little like the admin office of an all-girls' school. Not a lot of single guys come in to check out books."

"I'm just not ready to settle down," Laurie said. She slid one mile-long leg over the other. It might have been easy to hate her for her supermodel body and bright smile, but the fact was, she was funny and friendly. "Maybe because I'm lucky enough to meet men all day long. I'm a sales rep for a party supplies company."

Party supplies. Of course animated and attractive Laurie was a sales rep for a party supplies company.

"So they're out there—single men, I mean?" Emily asked. "From my side of the librarian's desk, I've sometimes wondered if they're a figment of the imagination just like the people inside the books in the Fiction section."

Laurie waved a hand. "Dozens. Every one of them looking for a good time."

Emily smiled a little. "Sounds familiar."

"Lots of them are great guys. Really." Laurie scooted closer to the edge of her cushion. "A group of us are having a big barbecue at the park this weekend. I'll be there, Gail here, too. You should come."

"Oh. Well…" Emily hemmed and hawed. It wasn't that she was leaving her weekend open for someone else or anything. It was just that…

"You're new to town. I can introduce you to some men, all vetted, if you know what I mean. Not a one of them has ever worn a blue wig or twisted a balloon into a baboon."

"I knew I shouldn't have mentioned that," Gail muttered.

Emily had to laugh. "I don't want to impose."

"I know the perfect guy for you," Laurie said, then glanced over at Gail. "Carl Fletcher. Now he's not looking for a wife—"

"And I'm definitely not looking for a husband," Emily hastened to clarify.

"But Carl knows all the best restaurants in town and can be very entertaining." Laurie turned to her friend. "What do you think?"

Gail appeared to consider a moment. "Smooth,

but not too smooth. Pretty, but not too pretty. Great backside. I say it's a go."

"Still…" Emily wasn't big on fix-ups.

Laurie's gaze shifted to somewhere over Emily's left shoulder. "Speaking of pretty."

A quick glance back told Emily who had snagged the other woman's attention. Her stomach jittered as Will entered the room, looking lean and dark and not the least bit "pretty." As the only male in the vicinity, his virility stuck out like a thumb. An un-sore, very manly and handsome thumb.

Gail looked over at Laurie. "Are you still seeing him?"

Laurie didn't take her gaze off Will as she shook her head. "Not anything regular. Just a couple of times early in the summer. We both got busy. But I'm feeling a sudden itch to free up my schedule for Wild Will."

Wild Will. Emily's stomach jittered again.

The woman waved toward the doorway. "Will?" she called out. "Will! Over here."

What could Emily do, but paste a smile on her face and sit back while Laurie the party supplies rep played honey to Will's bee? It wasn't long before he was leaning in for a taste, bussing the blonde and then Gail on the cheek, then glancing toward her couch. Upon catching sight of her, he halted a moment, then replayed the friendly greeting by brushing his lips just to the right of Emily's.

"Em," he said, his hand squeezing her shoulder. "How are you?"

Laurie's eyebrows were halfway to her hairline. "You two know each other?"

"Old friends," Emily hastened to say, before Will might think she'd try to stake a claim. *Wild Will.*

He took a seat beside her, and she tried not to stare at his hands where they rested on his knees. But it was impossible to ignore them altogether, because she so well remembered their lean length molding her breasts and sliding over the curve of her thigh.

Squeezing her legs together and tucking into the corner of the sofa, she tried to make herself smaller as the others chatted. It wouldn't do for any of them to notice the flush that must be crawling across her face or the odd tightness in her chest.

But she could smell Will! Even from a cushion away she could detect his particular scent and it conjured up all the kinds of images that made a woman warm and breathless.

Will, shirtless.

Pantless.

Naked.

Will, crawling between her splayed thighs, a wicked smile curving his mouth as he bent his head to kiss the inside of her knee. Goose bumps had raced from the spot, running toward the finish line, taking her closer to—

"Emily's coming."

She started, jolted from her sensual reverie by Laurie's voice. "What?"

"To the barbecue on Saturday," Laurie said. "Remember?" She wiggled her eyebrows and though she didn't add anything more, Emily knew she was signaling to her about the fix-up. With Carl Fletcher, who was pretty but not too pretty.

Laurie directed her attention back to the man beside her. "You come too, Will. We'll have fun."

Which was exactly what Wild Will wanted, right? He glanced over at Emily, his expression unreadable. "I don't know—"

"Of course you have to be there. It's at the park right around the corner from your house. And I'm bringing something new for us to play," Laurie said. "With these sort of wicket-like things. You throw lengths of rope at them that have ping pong balls on each end."

"Yeah?" That caught Will's interest. "I think I saw someone bring that set-up to a station house party one time. I didn't get a chance to try it, though."

"Well," Laurie said, crossing her long limbs again. "On Saturday will be your opportunity to play my game."

Emily still couldn't hate her, even with the supermodel legs and the phone sex operator purr. Because the other woman wasn't doing anything wrong. The blonde didn't have any idea that two nights ago Will had taken his old friend into his bed. All she knew was that this good-looking guy had Saturday free and that they both liked to play.

Will glanced over at Emily.

She gave a little shrug and directed her gaze at Laurie, the not-ready-to-settle-down party supplies rep.

"Sounds like an afternoon," Emily murmured, just loud enough for him to hear, "made in Wild Will heaven."

Will noticed Emily's arrival at the park the instant she showed up. He noticed it because he noticed a couple of the guys standing nearby straighten their posture and share a speculative glance.

"Fresh meat," one said. "Nice."

He turned his head to check out who they meant, and then felt a little burn grind in his gut as he realized they were referring to Emily. Emily, in a too-brief floaty skirt, a skinny-strapped sleeveless top, and a pair of cherry-red flip flops. Her toenails were painted the same color.

"I'd like a taste of those toes," the other man standing nearby said.

"Me, too," his buddy agreed.

"Hey," Will protested. Geez. This was Em, his childhood friend they were talking about as if she was a new item on a familiar menu.

The men shot him identical puzzled looks. "What's up? You have some prior claim on the new treat?"

Fresh meat. Tasty toes. New treat. Was this the way unattached men looked at the women strolling through their world? Okay, yeah, he knew that attitude had always been there, but now…now… Well, Will had *sisters,* damn it, and the notion that they, not to mention Emily, could be looked upon with such— well, what the hell would you call it but disrespect?— suddenly was ticking him off.

"Wild Will?" the man prompted again.

Wild Will. God, he was starting to hate that nick-name. But he was distracted from protesting it by the familiar note of Emily's perfume drifting close. And then she was there, standing beside him, wearing a sunny smile that just rubbed his bad mood the wrong way.

"Hi, Will." Her friendly gaze moved to include the two guys, too. "Um…hi."

"Hi," one replied, then shot Will a glance. "Going to introduce us?"

"No," Will said, grabbing Emily's elbow and hauling her away from them.

She gave out an uncertain laugh as he dragged her toward the coolers filled with soft drinks and beer. "Is everything okay?" she asked.

"No," he said a second time. Because he'd promised himself he wouldn't do this. He'd come to the barbecue to have fun, to mingle and be social, and not attach himself to Emily. He was in his bachelor mode, of course, and she seemed as easy-breezy as a man could hope, despite the fact that they'd been to bed together.

He glanced down at her and had to swallow his groan. They'd been to bed together. Why couldn't he get that out of his mind? It looked as if she had, he thought, as she rummaged through the ice for something to drink. When she bent over, her lightweight, swishy skirt molded to the curves of her very-fine behind, and he remembered holding those warm, smooth cheeks in his hands as he tilted her hips in order to penetrate her more fully.

God, he'd been inside Emily, and it was as if she'd climbed inside him and he couldn't get her out. Her perfume was in his head, the sound of her sweet, pleasured whimpers in his ears, the sight of her mouth, rosy from his kisses, was front-and-center in his memory.

"There you are!" A new voice snapped his attention away from his wayward thoughts. There was Laurie, the blonde he'd dated early that summer. While she gave him a wide smile, it was Emily she was addressing. "I've been looking all over for you."

"Just got here," she said. "What's up?"

"You remember my little plan." Laurie's expression turned sly as she flicked her glance at Will then back to Emily. "Are you ready to leave your old friend in order to meet a new one?"

"Sure," Emily answered with a little shrug. "That's what I'm here for. New friends."

Relaxing a little, Will idly watched as the two women wandered off. Laurie had tossed him a throaty and promising, "See you later," but Emily hadn't even wiggled her fingers his way. He wasn't bothered by that, though.

What bothered him, he decided a second later, was that Laurie had marched Emily right up to Carl Fletcher. Carl Fletcher! The dude was as blond as Laurie. What real man had hair the color of butter? He had a confident smile that proclaimed him the pampered progeny of orthodontists.

Since Will had personally paid the husband and wife team of Doctors Fletcher the cost of elephant upkeep to get five sets of identical Hollywood smiles for his younger siblings, it wasn't the grin that made him suspicious of the other man. It was his reputation.

Paxton, California, was a mid-sized city with a small-town grapevine. And face it, firefighters talked. Not just to their spouses or significant others, but also to many members of the community in the course of a day. And to each other. Between calls, when cleaning the engine or cooking a meal, they entertained themselves by yammering on about this and that. Sports, cars, movies…

Okay, and also about who was seeing whom, who wasn't seeing who any longer, who shouldn't be allowed near any woman who wanted to keep her panties on, even though the ladies somehow thought he was Mr. Nice Guy.

That would be Carl Fletcher.

The same Carl Fletcher who right now was enclosing his paw around the hand of new-to-the-area Emily. She was smiling up at Carl as if he wasn't trying to eyeball her breasts, which he was, damn it. Will tightened his grip on his beer and training his sights on the pair, started in their direction.

A hand landed on the center of his chest. "Where are you off to with that frown on your face?" Laurie asked. "I was coming back to talk. I've missed you."

He blinked down at her. She was Barbie-doll beautiful, with yards of blond hair, light blue eyes and a body that seemed made for the skin-tight little dress she wore. No flippy, flirty skirt for Laurie, her clothes hugged tight to every sleek line and each generous D-cup.

She looked perfect…

For someone else.

Over the top of her head, Will caught sight of Carl laughing with Emily as he reached out a hand to tuck a piece of her shiny hair behind her ear. That burn in Will's gut intensified. "What's up with you and Carl?" he asked.

Laurie's eyebrows rose. "What?"

"Why are you pushing other women toward him?" Because Laurie and Carl were a matched set. Single Girl Barbie and Swinger Dude Ken, both slick, both energetic, both bouncing along without an interest in deep emotions or lasting attachments. "You'd be great together."

A dull red climbed up Laurie's neck. "Did he say something to you about me?"

"No." Bouncy Laurie didn't look so carefree at the moment. Will narrowed his gaze. "Are you okay?"

"Of course," the blonde scoffed. "A few months ago there was a rumor going around that I had some sort of…thing for Carl, but it was entirely untrue."

Yeah. Sure.

Laurie glanced over her shoulder. "I want to be certain he understands it was a complete, um, fiction. So when I met your friend Emily, I thought introducing him to someone else would seal the deal. Show him I'm heart-whole and fancy-free. You know."

"I guess I do now." Fun-and-Frolic Laurie had fooled him, but good. While he could have sworn she wasn't any more interested in tying herself down than he was—not to anyone—from the flush on her face and the worried line between her eyebrows, the woman was a goner for Carl. "Are you sure he isn't, um, flattered about that little 'fiction' that was running through the rumor mill?"

She shook her head. "Absolutely not. Carl, he's... well, he's a nice guy..."

No, he wasn't.

"But you know him," Laurie continued. "He strictly plays the field."

Now it was Will's turn to frown. "Yes, I do." Keeping Count Carl was what one of his close buddies called him, and at the moment he was beaming all his Ken-doll charm at Emily. Emily, who was beaming right back up at him.

"Excuse me," Will said, without taking his gaze off the other couple. Then he headed straight for them.

They didn't interrupt their conversation when he strode up, so he did it for them. "Hey, Em, can I see you a moment?"

Surprise showed on her face, and she didn't look exactly agreeable, so he did what he'd promised himself he wouldn't—he attached himself to Emily by grabbing her hand. "I need to talk to the lady for a sec, Carl," he told the other man, and then hustled her away from Mr. Keeping Count.

The park was the oldest in town, with grass and trees, and a creek running through it. A meandering asphalt path led to the playground established at one end with swings and slides.

"What's going on?" she asked, as he towed her across the expanse of lawn. "Is there a problem between you and Laurie? You're acting very weird."

Will didn't dare let go of her. "I'm acting on your behalf, okay?"

"I have no idea what you're talking about." Emily planted her feet in the grass so that he was obliged to stop, too. Pulling her arm from his grasp, she stared up at him. "Will?"

He forked a hand through his hair, feeling as awkward as he had when explaining to Tom about the birds and the bees. "Look. You should probably keep away from Carl."

"Huh?"

This time he shuffled his feet. "He's…you know."

"What?"

"Dangerous?" Too late, he remembered how he'd promised to be Em's danger that evening in his bed.

Emily blinked. "Dangerous how?"

When he hesitated, she persisted. "An arsonist? A communist? A…I don't know…pugilist?"

"Of course he doesn't hit women," Will finally said. "But he hits *on women.*"

"Lots of men hit on women, Will. It's not a high crime. Not even a misdemeanor. As a matter of fact, it's usually how a man and a woman start to get to know each other. One says something, even, gasp, something flirtatious, and then—"

"This is beyond flirtation, okay?"

Emily shook her head. "Will, give me credit for some experience, okay?"

"But—"

"I'm not one of your sisters."

One part of him wished she was. Then he'd feel free to lock her up in her room, instead of having to reason with her. "Emily…"

"Later, Will." Sidestepping, she made to move around him and head back to the knot of people that included Keeping Count Carl.

Will blocked her way. "Listen to me."

"Why should I?" She jammed her hands to her hips and sparks glinted in her eyes. "You—"

"He's a horndog, okay? One of those kind of men who are into the conquest, but not what comes after. Carl's been through more women than my household used to go through tissues during cold season."

She rolled her eyes. "Will—"

He put his hand on her shoulder. "I don't like him, Em."

Her gaze went icy. "Why not? You just said it, didn't you? He's one of the kind of men who's into the conquest, but not what comes after, right? He's a 'horndog', correct? Isn't that exactly the goal you've set for yourself?"

His suddenly lax hand slid off her as she stomped off. She was eight feet away by the time he could feel his tongue in his head. "Em!" Sprinting, he took off after her.

She glanced back, and then totally missed the

small ledge where grass gave way to the concrete sidewalk. With a little cry, she stumbled in her cherry-red flip flops and fell to the rough gray surface.

And though he'd promised himself to stay unattached—to Emily as well as anyone else—when he hauled her up and saw that there was red blood welling from her palm, her knee and even from a scrape on her chin, blood as bright as those cherry-red sandals, he found that he couldn't let her go.

Chapter Nine

Under protest, Emily allowed Will to whisk her away from the park and around the corner to his house. Claiming she could use paper napkins and water-fountain water to clean up the damage from her fall had not made a dent in his determination. The stubborn man had even insisted he drive her and her car the short distance to his driveway.

But when she got inside his house, and caught sight of herself in a mirror, she understood his point a little better. Besides the raw knee and gashed palm of her hand, the blood had run down her neck from the injury to her chin and there was more than a little gritty dirt sticking to the tacky red stuff wherever it was starting to dry on her skin.

She had to whimper a little at the mess her clumsy tumble had wrought.

Will's hand tightened on her waist as he ushered her into his kitchen. "Hurting, honey?"

"Mostly my dignity," she admitted. She was irked that the accident had meant leaving the barbecue. Getting out in her new world, meeting new people, all of this was exactly why she'd left her hometown after her mother's death. A fresh start was what she'd needed to get her moving on from her grief and out of the little mousehole she'd made for herself in her hometown.

Will pushed her into a chair at the table. "I don't think I have dignity bandages, but I have all others known to man—sporting everything from superheroes to spring daisies."

"What about ones a little more inconspicuous? I don't want to return to the park looking like I'm eight years old."

One of his brows rose and he took on a big brotherly tone. "Why? You afraid Wonder Woman on your chin will leave you dateless next weekend?"

She restrained a roll of her eyes. His overprotective behavior, no doubt well-practiced during the years as the oldest sibling of younger sisters, only served to annoy her. "No comment."

He shrugged a shoulder. "I'll be back with the first aid kit in no time."

On his way out of the kitchen, his gaze lit on the answering machine sitting on a nearby countertop. She followed his look and noticed the blinking, message-waiting light. He pressed the play button as he ducked out of the room.

"Will!" Right away Emily pinned it as his sister Betsy's voice. "You were at Jamie's the other night. How come you can go by her house, but you can't come over and visit me? I've asked you fourteen-and-a-half times to drop by to see how well mom's quilt looks hanging on my living room wall." She huffed out a sound of irritation. "And if you can't figure out what that 'half' of fourteen-and-a-half refers to, it's the hint I'm leaving right now that you ASAP visit your adoring—okay, and annoying—cupcake-baking little sister."

As Emily smiled, Betsy's voice turned to wheedle. "Chocolate, Will. With chocolate frosting. Much tastier than those ones you bring home from the bad-food aisle at the grocery store and are probably right now in the cupboard next to the fridge."

Emily knew those cupcakes. Will had brought a suitcase's worth of them to camp every summer. Darting a look in the direction he'd gone, she popped up from her seat and snuck into the cupboard next to the fridge. Gold!

Without a guilty qualm, she brought a package back with her to her chair and dug in as the next message started playing. "Yo, bro. Alex here."

Will's brother, Alex, the only Dailey male sibling missing the night of her spaghetti dinner. Already Emily was predicting what he would have to say, and she discovered she was correct.

"So you had dinner with Max and Tom? What am I, chopped liver? You couldn't take me up on that run-and-a-bagel I suggested last Wednesday morning? And I was going to give you this great stuff for rubbing out scratches in auto paint. It'll get rid of that ding Betsy-Wetsy left last spring when she borrowed your truck."

Will walked in, a towel over his shoulder and a plastic case the size of two shoe boxes in his hands as his brother finished up his message. "Dude, call me."

Emily lifted her eyebrows at her host. "You've had some good offers there. Your brother can get rid of a scratch on your truck. Your sister will make you cupcakes."

His gaze dropped to the cream-filled concoction she'd half-demolished. "Looks like I might need some."

Without hesitation, she popped the rest in her mouth. "That's why I'm eating 'em," she said, once she swallowed the cake and frosting down. "I consider it my duty to bring about a familial reconciliation."

"My siblings and I aren't in any kind of conflict,"

Will said, yanking out a chair and then dropping into it to face her. He took hold of her injured leg and drew it over his knees so he could tend to her wound.

All right, she was a wimp, so she closed her eyes and reached for the package's second chocolaty treat as he went to work. "You're still working hard to keep them at an arm's length, though."

It cracked her heart just a little, that distance he was insisting upon between himself and his family, though she didn't think there was much chance that Will was going to have continued success with it. Not only did his brothers and sisters seem relentless, but there was Will himself. What kind of man took it upon himself to interrupt his afternoon and take a friend home in order to tend to her minor scrapes and bruises?

A caring man, who would sooner or later figure out that those sibs he considered so burdensome were actually pretty special.

Thinking of them and how much they cared about their big brother, that crack in her heart widened a little more.

"You know what I think, Will—" She gasped, interrupting herself as the sting of antiseptic met raw skin. He did the same to her hand before she got her breath back.

Bandaged on both places, she glared at him. "You did that on purpose."

"It was either that or stuff another cupcake in your mouth and I'm damn protective of my stash."

"You're protective, period," she grumbled. "I haven't forgotten, by the way, your silly little scene at the park regarding Carl Fletcher."

"Keeping Count Carl," he murmured.

"What?"

"Never mind," he said, then set her foot back on the floor and scooted his chair closer to hers. "Now it's time to clean up that chin." He lifted the damp towel he'd set on the table.

"You know," Emily said, leaning back. "I can do it myself."

He grabbed a handful of her hair to tug her near again, and without waiting for permission, went to work removing the blood that had trickled toward her throat. Gently.

Who could be annoyed at a man with such a soft touch?

His voice was soft, too. "You have chocolate on your mouth," he said. "You look like you did at fifteen when you stole into my cabin and found my hidden cupcakes."

Embarrassed, she ran her tongue over her lips. "There? Did I get it?"

His gaze was focused on her mouth. She saw his nostrils flare and she wondered if he could feel the suddenly racing pulse in her throat through the towel.

His hand released its grip on her hair to stroke it instead. "Emily…"

Then he sucked in a breath and let both his hands drop as he edged back on his seat. "So tell me what you've been doing with yourself this week?"

She gazed down at the bandage on her palm. "Quite a bit, actually. I've been taking yoga every morning at the gym I joined—hope my fall doesn't slow me down—and I went out for coffee with one of the other women from class before work yesterday."

"A new friend already," Will commented, a smile flitting over his face.

"I also officially joined Jamie's book club, which gave me an idea for something to start at the library. A movie club for teenagers…with tie-in books to get them reading more as well."

"Great." Will appeared even more pleased. "You'll meet a lot of people through my sister and that teen thing sounds like fun."

"Yeah." She gave a little nod. "I'm in e-mail contact with a film studies professor at the local community college. He's interested in being involved and we're meeting for drinks next week to discuss the possibility."

Will went from happy to uneasy in the blink of an eye. "He? Who is this guy again and how much do you know about him?"

She shrugged, ignoring his meddlesome tone. "Not

much, other than he was recommended to me by my boss. He lives next door to her. That's why we're going out for drinks. To find out more about each other and what we might do with this teen program."

"Right, right." Will's expression smoothed out and he leaned forward again, this time with a can of antiseptic spray. "Close your eyes while I get this stuff on your chin."

"No," she protested, eyeing the industrial-strength can. "I'm fine."

"But cowardly," Will said. "Stop being such a wuss." But his hand was gentle again, as it touched her jaw to angle her face just so.

"Please hurry up," she grumbled, closing her eyes, bracing for the next sting and bracing against the way his caring attention seemed to be doing more work on her weakened heart. "I want to get back out there."

"You're doing that, aren't you?" Will murmured, as he administered a cold, smarting shot of spray. "You wanted to move to a new place, create a new life for yourself. You've gone a long way toward your fresh start already. I admire that, Em. I really do."

She felt the press of an elastic bandage against her skin and she opened her eyes to see Will close up. Close up, and not moving away. He cradled her face in both of his hands as he studied her, his expression unreadable.

"What about you, Wild Will?" she asked softly. "Have you made any progress on your own goals?"

His mouth turned upward in a wry grimace as his gaze drifted to hers, then dropped back to her mouth. Her heartbeat sped up again, and heat flashed over her skin, setting her wounds to throbbing…and other places, too.

"My goals…" Will started, then sighed. "When I'm around you, I have to admit, Em, they seem to get all scrambled up."

"Will…" she cautioned, as he leaned forward.

"Shh." One finger pressed the center of her lips as he came nearer. "Let me. I just have to kiss and make it better."

The warm, light touch of his lips to her bandaged chin was not the least bit sexual. But all the same she felt it like a spear of sweet heat heading straight toward her toes. Her hands came up to clutch his wrists, but she didn't pull them away. She didn't move away.

Instead, she moved in for a real kiss. The sound of the quiet groan he made as she mimicked his gentleness, only lip-to-lip this time, went straight to her chest, finding that new crack and pushing it wider. The sure signal that she affected him as much as he affected her wiggled its way into her heart, causing an inner voice to warn about danger that the rest of her refused to heed.

"Emily…" Will said her name against her mouth,

and then again as his lips drifted across her cheek. He rubbed his face against her jawline and she felt his eyelashes brush her warming, sensitizing skin. Goose bumps ran for cover, dashing down her neck and under her tank top.

In reaction, her breasts swelled and her nipples tightened. Will speared his fingers through her hair and went back to her mouth, adjusting her head so that the slant of his mouth could achieve a tighter, deeper fit.

"Better than any boy's dream," he murmured, lifting his head to look into her eyes. His forehead rested against hers. "You murder the man," he said. "I admit I'm slain."

"Victim to my charms?" The thought delighted her, and she moved her mouth to kiss him for bringing up the idea. Librarian Emily, the girl who'd stayed home on prom night, the woman who'd holed up on weekend evenings with her stack of to-be-read books and her fantasies of summers long past, really had a fresh start here.

She was slaying a man!

And it was Will.

"I want you," she said to him.

He blinked, then a slow smile curved his mouth. "Yeah?"

"Yeah." Why couldn't she, why shouldn't she want him? Why couldn't she say it straight out loud? The new Emily she was now wasn't the same as the predictable, overly cautious, dry-as-dust Emily that she'd been in her hometown. And furthermore, she'd already been through where wanting Will would lead her and the result had been spectacular. Not only had the fireworks been a fabulous mix of fire and dazzle, but they'd been able to get up and go on just as before.

So why not again?

After the first time she'd been, well, smug, as she'd already acknowledged, and his Wild Will aspirations had not been compromised, had they? As a matter of fact, maybe they could put them to good use...

"I've been thinking." She cleared her throat and peeked at him from under her eyelashes. "A man who aims for 'wild' in his appellation—"

This time Will's groan was several notches louder. "What do I have to give you not to bring that up ever again?" he asked, scooping her from her chair and depositing her onto his lap.

He was warm, smelling of soap and sunshine and...Will. She snuggled against his chest because it seemed like the most natural place in the world for her to be. "Oh, come on. I think it's time you showed me your best untamed moves."

Groaning, he edged up her chin with a finger beneath her bandage, lining up their mouths so he could give her the kind of kiss that definitely earned an untamed rating. His tongue slid into her mouth, warm and wet, and Emily squirmed on his lap, trying to find a way to get even closer to him.

His hand left her face and moved to the ankle of her uninjured leg. He trailed his touch up her shin, then swept it back down, creating another wash of goose bumps that headed toward her knee, then northward. Emily squirmed again, pivoting to wrap her arms around his neck and rub her aching breasts against his hard chest.

Will's exploring hand stole beneath the hem of her skirt, his warm fingers lighting fires along the ticklish flesh of her thighs. Emily parted them—she couldn't help herself—and when he touched her over her panties, she jerked against him. He broke the kiss, sliding his hot mouth to her ear. His teeth closed on the lobe just as she felt his firmer touch tease her right where she throbbed for him.

She responded with liquid heat, and she realized he could sense it as he followed the curve of her body and widened her legs for his hand. "You do want me," he whispered, the hoarse tone rubbing against her nerve endings in yet another kind of touch. "I love to feel you, feel this. Feel that you really want me."

One finger tucked under the leg band of her panties and she whimpered as he stroked the heated flesh there. "Oh, Will." She wriggled her bottom on his hard thighs, and then ran her teeth along the edge of his jaw.

"Oh, Em." There was a smile in his voice and she

tried brushing it away with a kiss. But he took it over, turning it into something hotter, deeper. His tongue thrust into her mouth at the same moment his long finger thrust inside her.

Emily froze on a small gasp, startled by the sudden intimacy.

Will whispered against her mouth. "Too much?"

Her inner muscles answered for her, clamping down on him as she pushed her tongue into *his* mouth. He groaned.

"Too much for you?" she teased, empowered by the rough sound and the ready feel of his erection, hard and stiff against her hip.

He slid his hand free of her. "We'll see who surrenders first," he said. "Let me know when you can't take the heat, honey."

With that, he shifted her on his lap, drawing one of her legs over his hips so she straddled him, and so that their chests were flush. Her damp panties were pressed against the ridge beneath his jeans.

"Will?"

"Calling uncle already?"

"No." She ran her palms up his chest, her fingers finding the hard points of his nipples. Though she didn't have Will's wild ambitions, his body, his reactions destroyed her inhibitions. It was daylight, in his kitchen, and yet beneath the hem of her skirt they were pressed intimately together.

It got even more daring and more intimate as he tugged at the stretchy bodice of her tank top to bare her breasts. The skinny straps pinned her arms to her sides and her nipples stood out, flushed and tight, and she saw his eyelids take on a sensual droop as he stared at them. He licked his lips, and then he bent his head, sucking one nipple into the hot confines of his mouth.

Emily arched, pushing against him so that his mouth widened to take in more of her flesh. She cried out with the pleasure of it, her fingers flexing against his T-shirt covered chest. He backed off for a minute to yank himself free of his shirt, and then his flesh was bare for her touch, too. She palmed his pectoral muscles as he went back to tonguing and sucking on her nipples.

Her head fell back, and she rocked against him, forced to move by the absolute goodness of his insatiable mouth and the need that was tightening all the muscles in her body. His hands snuck under her skirt again, and the sensitive flesh on her inner thighs twitched as he stroked them. And then his touch was gone and she realized he was working on the buttons of his fly.

Heat sizzled through her bloodstream. He wasn't…? He didn't mean…?

Here in his kitchen? On the straight-backed kitchen chair?

He *was* wild.

His mouth made a path of stinging kisses from her breast, up her throat, to her ear. "Lift a little, honey."

Could she? Could she move? Could she do what he wanted *here?*

The smile he gave her was a teasing one, but the light in his eyes was fierce with burning desire. "I have a condom if you want to take a ride." The silky, hot flesh of his shaft brushed against her soft inner thigh and she suddenly—fiercely—wanted it all.

"You know I do," she whispered, her voice shaky.

His smile turned more feral. "Lift up a little."

When she did, he fingered away the crotch of her panties and then he was there instead, opening her.

Opening her heart.

Filling her.

Filling her chest with feelings that were half-remembered, and yet wholly new.

Under her skirt, his long fingers found her waist, and he directed her movements, encouraging her to slide down as he slid up. To roll her hips as he tilted his.

Theirs was a perfect fit: soft swells to hard planes, slippery heat to heavy thrust, masculine angles to womanly well.

Emily squeezed her eyes tight, trying to hold out, trying to hold on to this memory forever, but Will wasn't letting her off that easy.

"Open your eyes, Em," he ordered. "Look at us."

Look at them. Playing cowgirl and stud. Rowdy.

Maybe even a little raunchy. There wasn't another man in the universe who could get her, Librarian Emily, to make love in a kitchen in the middle of a Saturday afternoon. There wasn't another man in the universe who could make her do something that felt maybe a little bit dirty—and revel in every second of the sweet, hot sexiness of it.

He made her feel so safe.

"Come for me, Emily," he whispered, and one of his hands slid to the front of her body and circled and pressed and pressed and circled and her muscles clamped harder on the thick, satisfying intrusion inside her. She rode him, rode those circles of pleasure that spiraled tighter and tighter until she went…

Wild.

Wild for Will.

As her orgasm broke over her, her heart seemed to break open, already compromised by all the feelings Will brought out in her. Her chest ached as her body rocked and quivered. She let him take her mouth as he groaned in response to his own release.

She let him take her mouth, just as he had everything else. The sexuality that had been smoldering inside of her for so long was his. And so was her heart.

Maybe she could have grabbed it back if her wild lover hadn't been so gentle with her after. But the man who'd coaxed her to such an amazing completion in his kitchen now coaxed her into a warm shower. Then, once again bundled in his robe, he persuaded her between his sheets, where he held her against his damp, naked body, her head tucked into the curve of his neck and shoulder.

They dozed.

When she awoke he was putting a glass of orange juice beside her on the night table, and when he saw she was awake, he helped her sit up to sip the liquid. Then they snuggled together again, talking idly about everything and nothing.

She suggested he take his pizza skills up a notch by using pre-made crusts and his own toppings.

He mentioned she might find recruits for her film-and-book club through an outreach program the fire department had for teens.

They shared a lingering kiss.

It was a different kind of intimacy than they'd shared in his kitchen, she thought, rubbing her cheek against his warm, Will-scented skin.

And without a qualm, realized that her fresh start had led her back…back to an old love, now rekindled.

She was in love with Will. She glanced over at him, wondering what he thought of what was in store for them, and she caught him staring at her with an intent, considering expression in his eyes.

"What's on your mind?" she asked.

"I suppose we're heading for a divorce," he mused. "Surely an annulment is now out of the question."

Chapter Ten

Owen turned his head to stare at Will as they neared the first mile-marker of their favorite five-mile run. "You didn't really say that, did you?"

Will grimaced. Though he hadn't told Owen what preceded his words to Emily, he thought he could forgive a faux pas. His brain hadn't been fully engaged at the time. His head had still been reeling by what Emily had done with him in his kitchen and what high plane that erotic act had left him on. And then, with her curled up at his side in his bed, he could only keep repeating to himself, *I married this woman!*

And the lack of panic at that thought had…really sent him into a panic.

"I don't want to be tied down," he said to Owen. "God, not now when I've just gained my freedom. As for Emily…she's the same. She doesn't want to be tied to some old boyfriend from the past when she moved here to make a fresh start."

"Sounds good, friend," Owen agreed, then he paused. "But you didn't really say that, did you?"

"Oh, hell." Will hung his head so he could watch his running shoes slap against the asphalt. "Though she seemed to take it in stride, she left my place not long after. You don't know how much I wanted to kick my own butt after I heard the words come out of my mouth."

Owen grunted. "I know another butt that needs some similar tending to," he muttered.

Will shot the other man a look. Sweat had darkened his blond hair to a dull gold. He didn't look any happier than Will felt. "No luck reaching Isabella?" he asked.

Owen shook his head. "No luck at all."

His buddy had taken time off immediately following the Las Vegas trip. The Marston family were big-time big shots from way back and on occasion the other man slipped out of his fire gear and into a tuxedo to please his grandfather. Owen had spent the last two weeks fulfilling one of these command performances at the family's vacation home in Lake Tahoe.

"Izzy avoiding you?" Will asked.

"You think?" his friend said. "Damn it all!" He stepped up the pace and it took a burst of speed for Will to catch up with him. "What got into us that night?"

"And the night before," Will reminded him. He'd run into Emily on Friday afternoon and by Friday night both he and Owen had been sharing tables and kisses with the two women. It had seemed so easy, so natural, so exactly what he was looking for after all those years of sibling responsibility. A little sexy fun with an old friend.

A little sexy fun had turned into a lot of…

Hell, he didn't know what to term what was going on with him and Emily, or what he was going to do about it.

"Em e-mailed me the day after my stupid remark," he told Owen. "We can still actually annul our wedding. We just have to come up with something like intoxication at the ceremony. Or current insanity works, too."

Owen snorted.

Will could agree with the sentiment. Except, well, the nights he'd been with Emily in Las Vegas he *had* been intoxicated. With her scent, with the warmth of her skin, with the damn joy he'd felt in finding her again. Her mouth alone could make a man drunk.

As for current insanity…

She *was* making him nuts.

But that wasn't all on Emily. He slowed his pace because there was no running away from all this trouble taking hold of his life. "Call me a Luddite, but I'm thinking of dumping my e-mail account."

Owen snorted again.

In this day and age, yeah, he probably couldn't avoid an Internet-reliant life. But did he ever want to.

Avoid how convenient it was for those siblings of his to send him messages that dragged him back into the fold. "Jamie's called in her marker," he said. "Dinner on Thursday. No doubt the whole crowd will be there. But when she agreed to ask Em to her book group, I gave her an IOU."

"And she called it in."

"She called it in." He glanced at Owen. "Want to come?"

"Why? You need a buffer?"

"You'll be my second," Will admitted. "I invited Emily along, too."

Owen didn't need to say a thing for Will to know the other man was baffled. He couldn't explain it himself. "Look, if you come with us, you can grill Em about how to deal with Isabella."

"I think I'll work on my barbecuing skills all by my lonesome, thanks very much. Though I'm scratching my head at why you're setting up dates with the woman you want to be free from in the first place."

Will glanced down at the face of his sports watch,

noting the month and day. Once again he didn't attempt to explain his own fuzzy motives. He thought he could be forgiven for it because it was the time of year when nothing made sense to him.

Emily was comfortable at Will's sister Jamie's house. She was growing accustomed to his siblings, too, and the chaos surrounding the clan when the group of them got together. She wasn't at ease with Will, though. Not tonight.

Though she'd thought over that whole in-love-with-him thing and decided she'd been wrong about it. It had been a momentary lapse on her part, a little bit of her loneliness talking that had led her to believe she'd fallen for Will. The world didn't work that way, did it? It wouldn't be so unfair as to have a woman find herself in love with a man who wouldn't love her back.

So while she was in a better place about the emotional angle, it still wasn't going to be easy to have that long-postponed discussion about the dissolution of their marriage. It was definitely going to happen tonight, though, she thought, accepting the after-dinner mug of tea he'd retrieved for her and brought out to the deck at his sister's house. Sipping it, she studied him over the rim as he took a swallow from his bottle of beer.

Via e-mail, he'd asked her to accompany him tonight. Via e-mail she'd accepted. His second electronic missive had referred to the annulment and divorce information she'd sent to him earlier. "We'll get into this after Jamie's dinner," he'd written.

But despite Will being on the verge of getting what he wanted—her out of his hair—he didn't appear any more relaxed in her company than she was in his.

Maybe it wasn't about her, though. Maybe he was just soaking up tension from the general surrounding atmosphere. Because the Dailey siblings, while as loud and energetic as the other times she'd been around all or some of them, were palpably on edge. Throughout appetizers and then the dinner itself, they'd slid looks at their brother and at each other, as if they had something up their sleeves. Something that had to do with Will, and they weren't sure just how he'd take the surprise.

Emily's stomach jittered and she found herself stepping nearer to him, even as she knew the closeness wasn't good for her heart. Keeping her distance would be better, but once she breathed in the warm spiciness of his clean scent she found it even more difficult to move away. Will himself shifted, his arm grazing hers, and their eyes met.

"You look beautiful," he said. His voice was soft, but had a hint of accusation in it. "You always look so damn beautiful."

Yet instead of seeing herself as she was dressed

right now, in a pair of cropped jeans, sandals and simple, boat-necked white T-shirt, another image popped into her mind. Will, sitting in his straight kitchen chair. Emily straddling him, her little skirt draped over his thighs, hiding the secret, sexy business that was happening under the lightweight cotton.

Her nipples tingled, and she licked her lips, trying to solve the problem of a suddenly dry mouth. Will's eyelids dropped, his lashes hitting half-mast as he stared at her exposed tongue. Embarrassed, aroused, she popped it back in her mouth and lifted her tea. Maybe he'd think the flush on her face was due to the heat of the drink.

Shaking his head, he looked away. "That's one memory that won't be receding anytime soon," he muttered.

She might have laughed about the twin ways their minds worked, if only he seemed more appreciative than irked. So, yeah, some space was what they definitely needed. With a breath, she turned her back on him to smile at the little guy now marching onto the deck, plastic forks gripped in each fist.

"Are you helping Mom, Todd?"

Jamie's son nodded his head, continuing on his journey to the two long picnic tables where they'd eaten their meal. "We're havin' cake. Birt-day cake."

"Oh." Emily looked around the assembled crowd. "I didn't know this was a celebration."

The Dailey family quieted as one. This gathering was smaller than the first she'd attended—only the siblings themselves were present, without significant others, except for Jamie's husband, Ty, and their two children. They all looked at Emily, slid guilty gazes at Will, then looked down at their feet.

"What's going on?" Will asked, his voice sharp. "Nobody has a birthday this month."

Jamie stepped onto the deck from the house, a rectangular bakery box in her hands. "You wouldn't let us do anything for you earlier this summer," she said.

"This was all her idea," Tom added, jutting his thumb in his older sister's direction. It wasn't clear if he meant to give her the credit or the blame.

"I don't want to blow out any candles," Will said.

Todd rushed over to his uncle and strangled his knees with chubby arms in a sure sign of toddler adoration. "I do it."

"Both of us need to stay away from flames," Will said, leaning down to swing Todd up in his arms. "Right, buddy? Fire's dangerous. You need to remember that."

Emily's heart clenched a little at how naturally he held the boy and how sweetly the child nestled up to his uncle's chest. Despite how hard Will tried to separate himself from this family, every one of them, from the oldest sibling to his baby niece, Polly, wanted him in their lives.

Why didn't he see how special that was? Why didn't he appreciate their stalwart affection?

Jamie slid the bakery box onto the nearest table beside a stack of paper plates. "It's not really a birthday cake," she said. "Now, everyone, come back and sit down."

Again, there was that odd sense of tension on the deck. Dusk was settling, and Betsy had lit votive candles that sat in glass holders placed along the center of the wood surface. The group returned to the places they'd taken before, Will in the center, Emily beside him, his brothers and sisters arranged around the other places.

As he took his seat, Ty replaced Will's empty beer with a fresh one, and Emily looked up, trying to gauge the other man's expression. But the shadows and the flickering candlelight made it hard to get a clear read. Did he think Will needed some liquid relaxation for what was coming?

Because something *was* coming.

Will sensed it, too, she figured, because his lean body froze. "What's going on?"

Jamie had retrieved baby Polly, and instead of sitting, was standing behind her spot, shifting from foot to foot as the infant dozed in her arms. "It's nothing bad, Will. It was just something we thought...we wanted to acknowledge..."

Tom piped up again. "This was all her idea."

"Okay," Will said. "Jamie's the culprit. But what the hell's the problem?"

Todd craned his neck to look up at his dad from his place on his father's lap. "Yeah. What d'hell?"

It should have been at least a little funny. But nobody on the deck laughed.

Betsy cleared her throat. "It's not a problem, okay? It's something…something that has to be expressed. After thirteen years…I think it's time we told you something, Will."

Beside her, Emily felt his body stiffen.

Betsy continued. "You wouldn't let us talk about it at my graduation. You refused to let us have a party for your birthday this summer. But this month there's another important date—"

"No." Will's voice was tight and tension radiated from his skin. The little hairs on Emily's body lifted in empathetic agitation. "Don't do this," he said.

His youngest sister's voice rose. "Don't acknowledge and appreciate what you did for us? How you kept us together, a family? That's not right, Will."

Leaning over, she whisked the top off the box to reveal a fancy bakery sheet cake, chocolate—Will's favorite—with letters in blue that read:

Thank you, Bird Brother

"*Bird* brother?" Emily echoed.

A sheepish Max raised his hand. "That's on me. When I was learning to talk, I mangled 'big brother'.

It sorta stuck. We used 'bird brother' more often than his name until—"

"You didn't need to do this." Will made an abrupt rise to his feet. "You shouldn't have done this."

From his other side, Alex put his hand on Will's arm. "It's been thirteen years, Will. Thirteen years today. And—"

"I know what day it is," Will's voice lashed out and he jerked free of Alex's hold. "I know goddamn well what day."

"Ga-dan," little Todd repeated. "Ga-dan day."

"You hear that?" Will said, his voice still whip-tight. "You see what you're doing by bringing this up?"

"Ga-dan," Todd babbled. "Ga-dan day."

"Honey, shh," Jamie said to her son, then turned to her oldest brother. "Will, this isn't contributing to the delinquency of a toddler. This is us making sure that you know we know what sacrifices you went through all the years after Mom and Dad—"

"Stop!" Will hissed. One minute he was on his feet, pinned to the table by the picnic bench and the beautiful cake set before him. The next, he'd leaped the barrier behind him and was stalking off the deck, still holding his beer bottle. "Stay away from me. That's the only thanks I want. All of you stay out of my life."

Silence fell over the deck as they heard the front door slam. Will had gone.

Tom pointed to Jamie. "This was all her idea."

Todd lifted from his father's lap to peer at the dessert sitting on the center of the table. "Ga-dan day. Want cake."

Rising to her feet, Emily strained for the sound of Will's engine. It wasn't that she was worried about a ride home—surely one of the others would give her a lift to her house. She was wondering if leaving her behind was what he really wanted.

Well, of course leaving her behind was what he really wanted—they were supposed to discuss the dissolution of their marriage tonight after all. But did he want to be alone right now or did he need something else? A friend?

From what she could tell, out on the street an engine hadn't started up. So she took off in that direction. Jamie caught her eye as she passed. "Don't let him be alone tonight," the other woman said. "He's never been alone on the anniversary of our parents' death. I couldn't let it happen this year. We're always together, though we've never openly acknowledged it. This time I was trying to give the anniversary a better memory."

Emily nodded, but kept on going. This time, she decided, no matter how much he wanted distance from her, now wasn't the time for her to give Will any space.

Emily found him pacing the sidewalk outside his sister's house, his fingers still curled around his beer.

"Will…"

He didn't stop his agitated movement. "Let's go."

"You're upset," she said. "Your family is upset. Maybe you should go inside and talk—"

"Talk!" He swung around at her. "There's been too much damn talk about this. Let's go." His strides took him toward the driver's side of his truck.

"Will—"

"No!" With a fierce swing of his arm, he threw the beer bottle against the curb, where it smashed with a startling crash.

Emily froze, shocked by the violence and the sight of broken glass glinting in the glare of a streetlight. Then she looked over at Will and saw that he was paralyzed, too, his gaze trained on the mess he'd made in the street.

She found she could move again. "All right, Will. All right. Let's leave."

"Not yet." His hands forked through his hair, then he moved toward the broken glass with jerky strides. "God. The kids could be hurt. Todd. Polly. I need to clean this up. I have to take care of this."

Emily watched him gather up the largest shards, her heart falling into as many pieces. This was Will, the man who, despite his obviously roiling emotions, couldn't leave something dangerous that might possibly harm his nephew and baby niece.

I need to clean this up. I have to take care of this.

Will had taken on that responsibility thirteen years before and even in the throes of whatever was overtaking him now, that core of his wasn't shaken.

And neither was Emily's love for him, she realized. The idea that somehow she could rationalize it away or decide the unrequited nature meant it wasn't genuine wasn't working. Will was so much more than a childhood, summer romance, and she'd fallen in very real, adult love with the man he had become. With a sigh, she walked toward him. "Let me help."

"Stay back," he said. "I've already bandaged you once in the past week and I'm not risking another whiff of that antiseptic spray."

She didn't ask why. In her mind, it was an aphrodisiac. If it wasn't the same to him, she didn't want to know about it.

He didn't say any more either, and maintained his silence all the way back to her house. When he pulled into her driveway, he left the motor running and stared at her garage door as if it was a movie screen or maybe a tablet that held all the secrets of the universe.

Without thinking, Emily reached over and turned the key to kill the engine. "Why don't you come in? We'll have coffee. Tea. Water. Whatever you want." Whatever he needed. Because it was obvious that the stormy tension that caused him to throw that bottle hadn't dissipated. He was still strung tight.

"I'm no company for anyone tonight," he said, his voice terse.

"I'll chance it. Come inside."

She couldn't say what got him into her house. She only knew her rib cage relaxed a little from its constricting hold of her heart when he opened his door and followed her inside. He dropped to her couch, his knees spread, his elbows propped on them as he held his head in his hands.

Her heart stumbled. "Will." She sat down on the cushion beside his, her palm against his shoulder. She felt it twitch, but she refused to take it as rejection. "I think I know a little of what you're feeling."

He didn't lift his head, but his tone was belligerent. "Oh, yeah? You think you do?"

She didn't back down. "Yeah, I do. I lost my parents, too, remember?"

There was a charged moment of silence, then one large hand came up to squeeze hers, making her heart ache a little more. He sighed, his shoulders sagging. "Em…"

"Have you ever given yourself time to grieve?"

His head lifted. He stared at her. "Time to grieve?"

Made stupid by the odd expression on his face, she repeated it. "Yes. Time to grieve."

He laughed, but it was a short sound and not at all humored. "There wasn't time to grieve. I had to get on with it…get on with getting the kids to school, getting the food on the table, getting the bills paid, getting five kids grown up and launched right."

And he'd done that. He'd done it all, all that he'd just laid out for her. But still… "So you did those things. And now you have no reason to duck from why you had to do those things, Will. Thirteen years ago tonight—"

"Don't say it," he interrupted.

She had to say it. It had to be faced. "Thirteen years ago tonight, your parents died and you—"

There was no finishing the sentence. His hands were on her upper arms before she could get it all out, and he was jerking her closer, jerking her face toward his, busying her mouth with a kiss that was more about silence than about sweetness.

There was no sweetness in the kiss whatsoever. Who was he punishing? Her? Himself? Fate?

Still, his mouth against hers was hot and burning and the shiver that snaked down her spine was a tongue of flame. The kiss went on and on, until she couldn't breathe, but the desperation ignited new fires along her nerve endings and she swayed into the dizziness instead of pulling away from it.

When he lifted his head, the oxygen felt too pure. "Please," she whispered, wrapping her arms around him even though she didn't know what she pleaded for. "Please."

He got to his feet, taking her up with him. "Now,"

he said, the words guttural, his muscles still coiled with tension. "I need you right now."

"Will…"

"Let me," he said, his voice fierce. "Let me."

He'd said that each and every time, each and every time meaning, *Let me make love to you.* Now though…

Let him not think, was what he meant.

But why would she refuse? *What* would she refuse? This was the man she loved, and he was hurting. And the press of his flesh against hers, the new kiss he was giving her, sent all those heated, soft and swollen spots of hers throbbing.

They made it to her bedroom. And then they were naked, and then they were joined. His fingers twined with hers. He held her hands to the mattress and thrust in a driven, raw rhythm until she came. He buried his face against her throat and she felt him release…and she felt wetness on her neck.

She didn't comment on it, even as there was a telltale prickle at the back of her own eyes. She didn't comment on anything. Instead, she only held him closer to her as they drifted into sleep.

In the morning, she woke alone. There was a note in her kitchen, where he'd made coffee for her. The pot was full. He hadn't even taken a single cup's worth. She thought of that, that he'd wanted nothing more from her.

Then she looked at what he'd written.

His handwriting was clear. Stark. The pen black on white paper.

I'm sorry. I need to be alone.

And she'd bet all she owned that he didn't mean just for breakfast. Life *could* be just that unfair.

Chapter Eleven

After the evening meal at the fire station it was standby time, and the crew was free to do as they chose until a call came in. Though he wasn't much good at concentrating the last few days, Will joined Owen to study for the continuing education course they were taking on handling hazardous materials.

But it was a waste of time, because once the books were open and their notes spread before them, Will might as well have been staring at Egyptian cuneiform. Forking his hand through his hair, he groaned. "On nights like this, I'm glad I'm the only Dailey who didn't make it to college."

Owen looked up. "You could go now, you know. Your brothers and sisters are finished. The next tuition payment you make could be for yourself. You could learn something."

Will frowned. "What are you talking about?" He gestured at the work in front of them. "I'm always learning."

"The stuff you study is for the job. If you wanted, you could go to college and prepare yourself for another kind of job. A new career."

"A new career? Like what?"

"Anything, Will," Owen said. "You became a firefighter because there was a spot for you in the fire academy and you knew you could get through it quicker than a degree program when you needed money to take care of your family. Now you could prepare for any kind of career you want."

Will shifted in his chair, then slid his gaze around the room. The living quarters of the station house were comfortable. From the adjoining room, he could hear a couple of his buddies arguing about what to watch on TV. For those two it was the same-old, same-old—nature documentary versus do-it-yourself house project program. One of the other firefighters wandered behind Owen, flashing Will a distracted smile as she passed, her cell phone plastered to her ear. He didn't need to overhear a word to know Anita was talking her ten-year-old through his evening routine.

He knew his second family just that well.

Another crew member was in the kitchen, probably scarfing down one of the brownies that a grateful citizen had dropped by that afternoon. They'd saved her grandmother when the elderly lady had forgotten a pot on the stove. Besides getting the fire out and calling the ambulance for the disoriented homeowner, they'd hunted down the old woman's cat that had gone into hiding once the smoke alarm started shrieking. The look on Grandma's face when he'd held the pet so she could stroke it before the ambulance drove her off was worth every long night and every sooty day he'd ever had on this job that he...

That he loved.

Wow.

He'd been so damn busy working and raising the family that he'd never really given it much thought before. He loved his job.

It was a good thing to know, he decided. A good thing to be certain about. "I'm not after another career," he told Owen. "Now, an escape from Jamie and Max and Alex and Tom and Betsy...that I might go for."

Owen drew his notes closer and shuffled through the pile. "You could do it, then. You could move away and be a firefighter somewhere else. Start over, like your old friend, Emily, did in moving here."

Will opened his mouth, the instant refusal to leave his hometown on the tip of his tongue. Then he narrowed his gaze on Owen's too-carefully blank expression and leaned back in his chair, crossing his arms over his chest. "All right, you've made your point, for whatever reason you felt you needed to make it. I enjoy my job, I like where I'm doing it. So if you're so damn smart, why don't you come up with why I—well, I should say *we*—complicated the good thing we have going here by what happened in Las Vegas?"

For the life of him, he couldn't dredge up whose idea the wedding had been first. None of them had piped up with a single word of caution. And when Emily had stood beside him, her little dress hugging her curves and a silly veil perched on top of her head, he could only remember the smell of her perfume and that he was grinning like a loon and thinking he was the happiest—

Surely he hadn't been thinking at all.

He looked over at his best friend. "Well?" he demanded. "What's your answer? How could two smart, happy-in-their-careers-and-where-they-practice-them single men make the biggest mistake of their lives?"

Owen was still quite the Confucius with that no-expression expression. "Are you so sure it was a mistake?"

That left it to Will to provide the reality check. "Owen," he said. "The women we married ran away the morning after the weddings. You can't get the librarian who said 'I do' to say 'hello' to you now, not even over the stinkin' phone."

"I'm going to fix that," Owen answered. "I've got four free days coming after this shift. If it's the last thing I do, I'm tracking Izzy down."

Disquieted by the determination he heard in his friend's voice, Will leaned forward. "Owen, what are you talking about? You can't get Izzy to return your call." *And I can't get Emily out of my head.*

That unbidden thought sent his mind spinning off again. Not to Vegas this time, but to that last night they'd been together. The night of Jamie's awkward anniversary party.

When he'd realized what all the Daileys were gathered for, he'd been—hell, he didn't know. Furious, maybe, with a good measure of…something else he couldn't name thrown in.

He didn't want his siblings' gratitude. He wanted them to leave him alone!

Nobody understood it. Not even Emily. But that hadn't stopped him from demanding more from her, from demanding that she let him into her bed so that he could forget himself in her silken skin, her sweet smell, the soft, hot, wetness of her body.

Their passion had put them both to sleep, but he'd woken just past midnight, in an instant recognizing—just as he'd recognized that day at the Las Vegas hotel—that he was with Emily. There'd been that same sense of exhilaration, that same sense of rightness, and he'd not moved a muscle in order to leave her sleep undisturbed.

Her cheek was pillowed on his shoulder, and she was curled against him, her knee riding his thigh, her naked breast pressed to his side. He'd gone from semi-hard to poker-stiff, no surprise about that, but he'd ignored the automatic reaction to bare beauty in his arms to focus on less earthy sensations: the soft sigh of her breath against his collarbone, the silky feel of her hair against his cheek, the shiny quality of her fingernails as a trickle of moonlight found them resting against his chest.

That's right. He'd wallowed in the prettiness of the woman's fingernails!

God, he could see them in his mind's eye now, and didn't that just mean he had to, had to get a grip.

He had to get out from under the weight of the feelings he was beginning to have for her. Unless he did, they were going to take him down.

Across the table, Owen was frowning at his cell phone. Will straightened in his chair. "What's up? You heard from Izzy?"

"My grandfather," Owen replied. "Demanding another command performance, I guess, though he just had those two weeks of Marston togetherness in Tahoe and didn't manage to convince me then of the error of my ways."

What had once been a mom-and-pop feed and farm supply, Owen's grandfather had grown to a much bigger business. Owen's brother was ready to step into that side of things while his younger sister was eager to take over the winery the family also owned, but old Mr. Marston hadn't given up on getting his oldest grandchild under the company thumb, too.

Will had met the irascible, stubborn patriarch, but his money was on Owen. His friend looked up. "Damn it. Get this—the old buzzard has learned to text message. Next thing you know he'll have found out about what happened in Las Vegas."

"I thought what happened there was supposed to stay there," Will muttered.

Is that where they'd made their mistake? All four of them thinking it was a lark instead of legal?

But hell, none of them was that dumb. The night they'd wed on a whim, it hadn't felt whimsical at all. It had felt like a hell of a good idea.

But an idea that had run its course all the same, he told himself, as he pulled out his own phone. Without allowing a moment for second thoughts, he searched his address book then called Emily's number. Tonight they'd plan a course of action regarding what to do about this marriage business.

It was time, wasn't it? Owen was going to track down his wife, while Will was going to find his way out of the trap he and Emily found themselves in.

She answered on the first ring. "Eliot?" she said, her voice breathless.

Will lifted the phone to stare at it a moment, then he slammed it back against his ear. "Who's Eliot?"

"Oh. Will." She laughed a little.

What the hell was so funny? He cleared his throat. "Did I catch you at a bad time?"

"No, no. I just got back from drinks—"

"With Eliot?"

She laughed again. "Yes. He's that professor I told you about, and he forgot a book at the restaurant. I brought it home with me."

"You're dating a professor?"

"No, Dad." She huffed a little and he could imagine the annoyed expression on her face. "It's a business thing. Remember, the man who was interested in my film and book club idea?"

"Oh, that." Had he really sounded fatherly? Maybe he could live with fatherly. "Is this guy married? Is he a thousand years old?"

"He doesn't wear a wedding ring—"

"You and I don't either." Though when had Emily taken hers off? He remembered sliding it on under the approving gaze of Reverend Elvis, but he hadn't seen her wearing it since. "So how old is this Eliot?"

"He's thirty-five. Eliot spent a few years in Hollywood—actually starred on a soap for a while—

before realizing he'd rather teach about films than try to break into them."

Some pretty boy, wannabe actor had been out tonight having drinks with Will's wife.

Earlier, the idea of what he and Emily had done had felt like a weight he was carrying on his shoulders. But this, this idea that his Emily was out with someone else—would likely be out with other someone elses once they dissolved the marriage—felt like a pair of hands strangling him around the throat.

From the minute he'd seen her again, he'd done everything he could to tie himself to her—making sure that they spent every moment together in Las Vegas, not once balking at the crazy idea of marrying her, not even when he'd gotten a glimpse of the Bible-toting, bling-wearing Elvis. Now his throat was closing up at the idea of her with another man.

So tight he couldn't get out the words that would precipitate the end of their marriage.

"Emily…" His voice didn't sound like his own. "Emily, we have to—"

The alarm in the station house sounded. Damn. Another delay. He rose, his mindset already switching from personal to professional. "Gotta go, Em." If she responded before he clicked off, he didn't hear her voice.

* * *

It was a residential fire and even in the dark they could smell and see the heavy black smoke as they arrived. The home was two stories, a vestibule room attaching the living area to the garage. Over the wide garage entrance was a metal canopy extending out another ten feet. It appeared the fire had started in the vestibule and moved to both house and garage.

Dressed in turnout gear, helmet, hood, gloves, boots and self-contained breathing apparatus, the firefighters got to work. Owen and others from a second engine moved toward the house itself, while Will and Anita approached the open garage with a charged hoseline. Will had the nozzle in hand, Anita, carrying an ax, backed him up as they moved under the canopy and then into the garage.

He could see the flames had spread rapidly across the ceiling and assumed they were finding plenty of fuel in the enclosed attic area. Their hose was having some effect, though, and he only hoped that the others were doing as well in the house. The home-owner had met them out front and said the family had evacuated, so there were no worries about anyone besides his fellow firefighters.

When their SCBAs were running low on air, he and Anita backed out for a bottle change. After re-placing their cylinders, they went right back in and resumed putting water on the fire. He heard a muffled sound from Anita, but before he could look around, debris fell from the ceiling onto his head. The heavy thunk to his helmet sent him to his knees.

Damn. Holding fast to the nozzle, Will struggled back to his feet and didn't protest when Anita indicated they needed to get the hell out. Only three minutes into their second bottles of air and conditions were deteriorating.

Once again, they backed out of the garage door, but remained near the doorway and under the canopy. With the hose line still in operation, this time Will made a conscious choice to go to his knees so he could better direct the nozzle toward the fire consuming the garage ceiling.

Then, disaster. Without a breath of warning, the overhanging canopy crashed down. Metal slammed into Will's back, hitting his tank and knocking off his helmet. He fell to the concrete as heavy debris dropped. Imprisoning him. The dark was absolute. Smoky, and absolute.

Damn, Will thought again. *Damn and double damn.*

"Anita?" He called her name, but he didn't hear a reply and the wreckage enclosing him was packed tightly.

His mind kicked into emergency mode as his predicament more fully registered. The rubble and the metal overhang burying him were heavy, too heavy for him to simply stand up and shrug them away. He was on his side, one arm pinned, the other free. Free enough, thank God, that he could reach and activate the PASS attached to his SCBA gear. The personal alert safety system worked as designed, immediately emitting a loud audible alarm.

But hell if he was going to rely on that alone. The damn canopy and all that hadn't held it up were lying on top of him and who knew how muffled the alarm was to those standing outside. Of course the other firefighters would have noticed the collapse, but they'd have no idea where to start looking for him. So he added to the noise of the PASS alarm by pounding on the debris piled around him.

The exertion sweat he'd worked up during his firefighting had turned icy, he noted, and one of his ankles was started to throb. It could only mean the first jolt of oh-shit adrenaline was starting to wear off, and he gritted his teeth as he continued banging his fist on anything within reach. He stretched farther, trying to find a new material that might elicit a louder noise, and there, just a few feet beyond that, he thought he detected a small opening.

He could lie here, hoping someone could figure out where the hell he was under all this crap, or he could try to help them find him. One of his arms was still pinned, and it was a risk to move and chance the broken stuff settling even more dangerously on him, but Will had reason to make the attempt.

Because it came to him, suddenly, that he had to get out from under this. Jamie, Max, Alex, Tom and Betsy didn't need to lose another family member. His mind flashed on his nephew, Todd, twined on his leg. Even within his smoky prison, he could smell baby Polly's just-shampooed hair.

With a heave, he wrenched his trapped arm free. Nothing else around him moved. *All right, all right,* he told himself, *that's a sign.* The sign to go for it.

Taking a breath, he sent a last thought to his fire-fighting buddies who he knew were coming up with their own plan to free him. *Hang on, everyone.*

Bird Brother was on the move.

His pulsing ankle protested as he started crawling forward, but he ignored it. It was his SCBA tank that stopped him instead, catching on something lying on top of him. Will wormed around, shrugging and twisting as best he could in the tight spot until he could wiggle free of the straps of the SCBA. His face mask still in place, he scooted along on his belly, toward that promising chink in the debris. Elbowing his way through and around pieces of 2 x 4 and 2 x 6 lumber, he finally reached the opening. Sucking in the air from his tank—and how much of that was left?—he stuck his arm up into the night air and started waving it around.

That was the best he could do, he realized. The only thing left was to wait for rescue.

And think, he realized forty-five seconds later as a million jumbled thoughts clattered against each other inside his head. Despite the patch of night air above him, it was still damn smoky in his confined space and it was making his mental processes murky, too.

Dozens of snapshots appeared to him in the darkness, though. He could see them against the dark gray backdrop. The sibs, black matchsticks lined up at the double funeral of their parents. Brighter images, too—the chaos of their schoolwork spread over the dining room table, the tumbleweeds of Christmas wrapping littering the living room on holiday mornings, the raucous party they could make out of something as commonplace as one of Jamie and Ty's barbecues.

If he didn't get the hell out of here in one piece he wouldn't experience that again. If he didn't get the hell out of here in one piece, their big brother wouldn't be around to keep them in even a semblance of order. Would someone check the oil in Betsy's car? Who would pay attention to Alex's rants about his favorite sports teams? Would Tom ever realize he was drunk in love with his girlfriend Gretchen and would someone be there to pick him up if he saw the truth too late?

Emily showed up then in his mental scrapbook. He saw her in a bathing suit and little sarong. A wedding veil. That kicky little skirt she'd worn in his kitchen when she'd gone wild on him. He saw her in nothing but skin.

His breath stuttered in his chest. His imagination was killing him, he thought, but then realized his tank had run out of air. Thinking of his family, of Emily, he brushed off his face piece and lifted his head toward the meager showing of night sky he could see around his lifted arm.

Coughing a little, he waved his hand with more vigor. He'd felt trapped by all of them, by his brothers and sisters and by the woman he'd married, but now that he was trapped *away* from them—

Something touched his hand. Fingers. Another hand, grabbing his. Clasping it hard.

He'd been found. Relief eased the tightness in his chest, even as he coughed some more. He'd been found. The crew knew where he was.

Bird Brother was going to make it home to the ones he loved.

A firefighter's helmet blocked the little light coming through the hole in the debris. "We'll get you out of there, Will," a voice assured him. "But it's going to be dicey."

Bird Brother was going to make it home to the ones he loved…maybe.

Chapter Twelve

Emily discovered that she could make herself a mousehole wherever she was. For a while, starting with that moment of recognizing Will, through their impulsive marriage, and on to their brief affair, she'd thought she'd left behind the reclusive librarian she'd become in her hometown.

But since the morning she'd woken to Will's note, she'd found herself scurrying between her stacks of books in the library and then straight to the ever-growing pile of them in her house. Her mouseholes, her fortresses, the armor she kept between herself and getting out in the world.

Whatever you wanted to call her place of work and the place she called home, the result was the same. Emily was once again in full retreat from the *sturm und drang* that she knew were the unavoidable consequences of living life.

The brief meeting she'd had with the film professor that evening had been the exception, and she still might have congratulated herself about the event if her heart hadn't galloped like a runaway horse when she'd heard from Will soon after. And after *that,* after he'd had to break off the call, if she hadn't slipped into flannel pajamas, her thickest robe and a pair of hand-knitted slippers that had been her grandmother's and were probably fifty years old.

It wasn't even eleven o'clock and she was tucked into a corner of her couch with a cup of tea and her favorite comfort read.

Her phone rang.

She let it.

The sound cut off abruptly, before her answering machine could spit out its spiel, and she went back to her book. Now if her cell phone rang, she'd have to get up and take the call, since it was the number her boss at the library had, that Izzy had, that she'd given Will.

But Will had gone out on a fire call, Izzy was being stubbornly silent since the last time Emily had harassed her about getting in touch with Owen—and since she was still married, Emily didn't have much room to criticize, anyway. Her boss had never once called her during her off-hours.

No one else had the number. She cocked her head toward the kitchen, where the phone was plugged into its charger. Will might be back at the station already. He might want to continue the conversation they started...

But it remained silent.

And Emily settled into the comfortable sofa cushions and tried pretending she was a Regency-era miss instead of a modern mouse. This time it was a knock on her door that interrupted.

She started, and automatically half-rose, but then she dropped back to her seat. Who would come visiting at this time of night? Kids out on a prank?

Who had her address anyway?

Her boss, who hadn't called her cell phone.

Izzy, who was on the other side of the country.

Will, who was working a twenty-four-hour shift.

Glancing at the door as someone banged on it again, she double-checked that it was locked and deadbolted. She was safe. Safe in her mousehole, insulated from worry and heartache and all the highs and lows that had come to her over the last few weeks. The highs and lows of living life.

The next knocks were louder, a declaration of impatience and insistence. Really, who could it be? Not her boss, or Izzy, or Will—

"Emily!" A voice called out. No, not Will, but one of only two others who'd ever been to her house. One of Will's brothers.

Her heart clawed its way from her chest to her throat as she approached the door. "Max?" she called back, even before she had her hand on the lock. "Is something wrong?"

"Will." Max's voice was muffled. "It's about Will."

Her fingers slipped on the deadbolt. She clamped her teeth on her lower lip and focused on her hand, finally managing to turn the mechanism and fling open the door.

Cool air rushed over her colder skin, and Max faced her, his hands in his pockets and his eyes worried. A younger, leaner version of his brother. A more scared version. Even standing before an Elvis asking for his "I do," Will hadn't appeared afraid.

"What is it?" she asked, her voice hoarse. "Oh, God, what's happened?"

"I don't know exactly." Max's gaze bored into hers. "But something went wrong at a fire and we're supposed to get to the hospital. One of the sibs told me to stop and pick you up on my way."

"Pick me up? I'm not, he wouldn't..." Oh, God. Will wouldn't want her. They weren't anything to each other.

Max bounced on the balls of his feet. "Are you going to change first? Please hurry."

"I...I..." Unsure what to do, she gestured him over the threshold, then backed toward her bedroom. "We don't know if he's hurt, or...?"

Oh, good Lord, what was she dithering about? She turned and ran toward her bedroom, already stripping off her robe. In seconds she rushed back out and then she and Max ran to his car.

As they drove off, she looked back at her house, the lights she'd left on making it look cozy. Secure.

But knowing something had happened to Will—*not* knowing what had happened to Will, meant she wouldn't be safe there even behind another set of locks or even bars on the windows. Still, she'd discovered a knack for making mouseholes anywhere. Surely in the midst of the large Dailey family she could stay back—unnoticed and perhaps even invisible—thereby assuring herself all was well with Will. And without putting more of her emotions on the line.

Mouseholes were mighty fine for her, she'd decided.

The hospital's emergency room waiting area was filled with uncomfortable chairs, tattered magazines and people in various stages of misery. A child held an icepack to a cut lip, a grizzled old man slumped against molded plastic in an attitude of surly yet stoic patience, a gaggle of Dailey brothers and sisters roiled in a restless knot in one corner.

Max made his way straight for them, but Emily hung back even as she kept her ears open for news.

It didn't take long for both her and Will's brother to be filled in. A fire, a collapsed metal canopy, a search to find Will under all the wreckage.

Wreckage.

They'd had to cut him out.

Cut him out.

It took ten long minutes once they'd located him to free him from under the debris. Though he'd protested, they'd brought him to the hospital, because obviously he'd suffered from smoke inhalation and there was something wrong with his ankle.

Something wrong with his ankle. Smoke inhalation.

Emily's head felt heavy, as if someone had stuffed cotton wool in her ears. Her hand to her chest, she backed away from the circle of Daileys, needing to get away, get out.

At home there was a couch, a soft robe, a Regency miss at a dance.

"Emily!"

She froze, as Jamie's gaze found hers. The other woman strode through her family to take hold of Emily's arm. "They said we'll get to see him in a few minutes. He'll want you to be there."

Emily didn't have the voice to set Will's sister straight. So she let herself be swept into the Dailey midst, and then, a few minutes later, she was swept along with them toward the hospital room where Will lay.

The family gathered around the bed and then just stood there, frozen with concern. Emily huddled by the door. She stared at Will, noting the scrape on his forehead, the oxygen mask over his mouth and nose, the length of his body that ended with a wrapped ankle propped on a pillow.

She didn't think he noticed her as his gaze roamed over Jamie, who was cuddled close to her husband, Ty, then on to Max, Alex, Tom and Betsy. Will pulled the mask away from his face. "For God's sake, Tommy," he said, his voice hoarse but happy-sounding. "Are you crying? Betsy Wetsy I can understand, but—"

The rest of his teasing was lost as his brothers and sisters converged on his figure. All Emily could see from her spot by the exit was his big hand roaming over dark hair, patting a shoulder, pausing to let fingers clutch his.

"We thought it might be something bad." Jamie's voice came out muffled, as she was pressed, Emily supposed, to her brother's shoulder. "We thought you might have...have..."

"Left you rug rats?" he finished for her. "Then who would Max run to when he can't balance his checkbook?"

"Hey," a male voice protested.

"Who can actually get Ty's lawnmower started for him?"

"Hey," Will's brother-in-law echoed.

The family moved back, grins intact and each echoing the one stretched across their big brother's face. He gazed around them again. "You didn't think I'd leave you guys to fend for yourselves, did you? Knowing I had to keep the herd in line was what kept me determined to get out from under there."

The worry had evaporated from the Daileys like steam under a summer sun. They started chattering as they always did, everyone talking at once, everyone vying for Will's attention and approval. She smiled a little, knowing he was in good hands, and wondering if the gap between him and his family had finally been breached for good.

She wouldn't be around to know for sure, but he was safe, and she'd be safe, too, once she got back to her cozy house and her comforting book.

She pulled open the door, only to face a woman in a firefighter's uniform. Her hair was sweaty and her eyes were red and she looked past Emily to the man on the bed. Emily scuttled sideways to make room as she strode across the floor.

The Daileys, sensing the newcomer's presence, opened their circle so that the woman had a spot at the end of Will's bed.

"Anita." Will frowned. "What are you doing? You weren't hurt after all, were you?"

"No, no." She shook her head. "That canopy missed me. But…but it's been a bad luck night, Will."

He stilled. "What are you talking about?"

"Our guys were up on the roof of the house. Ventilating it." The woman cleared her throat. "It gave way, Will."

"Our guys." His voice barked out. "Our guys who?"

"Palmer, Palmer from Engine 8. He's dead, Will."

"Oh." Will slumped against his pillow. "Oh, God."

"And Owen," the woman went on. "Will, Owen went down, too. The ambulance just came in a few minutes ahead of me. I don't know how bad it is. But he's alive, I know that."

Will felt like he'd been hit in the head yet again. Oh, hell. Palmer gone, and Owen…? His gut clenched. *Bad luck night.*

"Will, I'll go downstairs and find out what I can," Alex said. "The woman at the reception desk looked as if she will respond to flirting."

Tom rose from his spot on the end of Will's bed. "I'll go with, in case she responds to good-looking guys instead of pushy ones."

Alex cuffed their younger brother, but the gesture was half-hearted. All the grins in the room were gone.

Jamie already had her cell phone out. "I'll call the babysitter and get her to give me Owen's sister's number. I know I have it somewhere. I'll call her to see what we can do to help."

Betsy grabbed Max's arm. "Max and I will…

we'll…I don't know, we'll do something useful. Don't worry, Bird Brother. We'll take care of things. You can count on us."

Max nodded, his gaze somber. "We'll take care of *you,* Will."

They all seemed about to leave. Suddenly, Will couldn't have that. The idea of being without them without saying something more, something else, set in a panic that made his head pound harder, his gut twist tighter. Though it was different, this need to be with them, different than when he'd been under that canopy, because suddenly he saw the whole picture.

He saw the whole thing about the Dailey brothers and sisters and him.

You can count on us.

We'll take care of you, Will.

"Wait, wait." The words burst out of his mouth and he grabbed the arms of the two closest. Betsy. Max. "I need to tell you guys something."

Five sets of Dailey eyes looked back at him, Ty was staring too, and Will gave them all a reassuring half-smile. "I knew you guys were all going to be here. Once the captain called Jamie."

Her returning smile was faint. "You know the family grapevine is a fine-tuned machine."

"And I counted on that," Will said. "I counted on that like I know every one of you counts on me. Like I hope you know you *can* count on me."

"Of course," Betsy said, her voice puzzled.

"Ty says you're the oil in the Dailey gears," Jamie added.

"Well, I'm glad to hear that. But everybody, everybody, the fact is, you're the oil in my gears, too. As much as you rely on me...I realize I rely on all of you right back."

Betsy dropped to the mattress beside him, tears in her eyes again.

Will squeezed her hand. "I relied on you being at the hospital tonight, I rely on your prayers for Owen. I relied on you guys this summer to give me space when I demanded it. But, thank God, not too much space."

"We could never do that," Betsy assured him.

He smiled at her, then looked around to catch the eyes of all the rest of his siblings as he thought of how they'd stepped up to help Emily when she'd first moved to town and how they were ready to do whatever they could for Owen. "You're not a weight around my neck. You're my tribe and you're my support and each one of you is even more precious to me now that I realize I can count on leaning on you, as much as you can count on leaning on me."

He ignored Jamie's sniffle because she always liked to think she was tough. "I was a flat-out idiot for wanting freedom from your love."

He heard another sniffle, louder this time, and realized it was Anita who was brushing away tears from her face. "'Nita, sorry to bring you in on the family drama."

"No," she said. "It's lovely. I feel...privileged. But I need to tell you one more thing, in case it rings a bell for you."

"What?"

"The guys said that when they got Owen out he was asking for an 'Izzy'. He kept saying the name over and over. Captain thinks maybe it's a dog he used to have, or something, but in case it's someone important—"

Will groaned. "Izzy's not a dog he used to have. But I don't know how to contact—"

"Izzy," a new voice interjected. "You don't know how to contact Izzy, but I do."

The crowd around his bed parted and there, standing at the back of the room and looking as if she wished she were anywhere else, was Emily.

Emily. God. Emily.

He'd been all messed up about her, too.

Ty took his sister's arm. "Let's go find out what we can see about Owen, people. Give Bird Brother here a few minutes to catch his breath."

Jamie yanked the oxygen mask back over his face, but he pushed it away again as his family, Anita too, melted away. This time he didn't stop them.

His chest felt tight, but it wasn't the lack of air that

was affecting him this time. It was the look on Emily's face. His Emily.

"I'm assuming the grapevine got to you, too." The smoke had roughened his voice.

"Max came to the door. I was in my pajamas, but he insisted."

Bless Max. Just another reason to feel grateful to his family. They knew to bring him Emily. Looking at her dulled a little of the edge of his sorrow over Jerry Palmer, and his worry about Owen. The sadness over Jerry would hit him again, he knew it, but he'd take the time to feel it, like he hadn't when his parents passed. Not until Emily insisted had he allowed himself to grieve.

She cleared her throat now, then plucked at her top. "I'm embarrassed to say I'm still in my pajamas. Half of them, at least."

He shrugged. "I don't care. You're here."

She didn't move from her spot by the door. "You, too. You're here."

Not dead, but he'd come close. Not injured, not really. He could see the knowledge of that on her face and in the wariness in her big blue eyes.

He remembered now, as clearly as if it had just happened, the one who had suggested they marry in Vegas. It had been *him*.

His instincts were good, he always knew that. Like Em, he only got into trouble when he over-thought things. "Come here, honey." He held out his hand to her.

She didn't move a muscle. Oh, yeah. His Em was thinking hard.

He coughed and when he saw the lines of concern crease her brow, he didn't try to hold back another round. His instincts said he should go with the sympathy if it gave him an advantage. This was just that important. "Em," he said, "please come here."

From her pace, he might as well have asked her to a hanging. Her own. He leaned forward to catch her hand, then drew her to the side of the bed.

"You're scared."

Her whisper barely sounded in the room. "I've never been so frightened in my life."

He squeezed her fingers. "It's okay though. I'm okay."

"I call my house my mousehole," she confessed, the words blurting out. "I'm safe there."

She was in full retreat, he could see that, and all because he'd stopped listening to his instincts.

"But I'm out here, honey." He rubbed his thumb over her knuckles. "I can't do much about that, because this is my job, what I'm good at. But out here, it rarely means anyone gets hurt. Honest. And out here we get to play together."

She frowned again. Okay, so "play" wasn't a good word to use.

"I don't know that we want the same things, Will."

"I want you."

The face she made wasn't flattering. "You want good times. To play." She looked down at their joined hands, and then back up. "And even then, you've run hot and cold on me, Will."

"I've run," he acknowledged. "But that was because you showed up when I least expected you, Em. I was all set to reclaim a life I thought I'd missed and there you were, everything I would want if I wanted to settle down."

"Which you didn't."

"I wanted to have good times. But, Em, guess what? Guess what I've discovered these last few weeks? You *are* my good times. Without you, I won't have times as fun or as passionate or as full of…love, as the ones I've had when I'm with you."

Color rushed to her face. "I can't help being in love with you."

Though he could tell she was a little mad about it. "I wouldn't want you to. Em—"

"Will, I have word on Owen." Alex stood in the doorway. "It's good news. He's injured, but nothing life-threatening."

A little of Will's tension eased. "Thank God."

"Thank God," Emily echoed. "Though I'm still going to get Izzy on the phone."

He looked back at her, then glanced at his brother,

trying to send him a silent message. There were things that needed to be said, in private, before she started making calls. Alex might have picked up on the unspoken communication, but just then Betsy and Tom drew up behind him. "Did you hear the news about Owen?" his little sister demanded.

"Yeah. So could you guys…"

Ty and Jamie arrived now too, shoving the other three into the room. Then, not that he should have been surprised, Max showed up, and it was another Dailey crazy chaos. They were exchanging information, their voices getting louder by the moment.

He was never going to get a chance to be alone with Emily, Will figured. Not while he was still in this damn hospital bed. Ah, well. His brothers and sisters had always been part of his package and he was done thinking that was a bad thing.

Yanking on the hand he held, he brought the woman he loved closer to him. "I've been a short-sighted idiot, Em. But I'm seeing clearly now. That means I'm going to insist you venture out, my mouse. Come out and play with me, sweetheart, because I love you and am not about to let you go after finding you again."

Miracle of miracles, the Dailey clan all stopped talking at once, so that his "I love you" and then all the rest rang loud and clear in the room.

They held their collective breaths.

He cupped Emily's cheek with his free hand. "I hope my boy's dream can be this man's future, Emily. I'm so in love with you. Will you please marry me?"

She blinked as tears welled in the most beautiful eyes on the planet. "Oh, Will. I was trying to do the Danielle Phillips thing again. You know, hoping that if I avoided you and how I felt about you it would all go away."

"But?"

"But she just stole my necklace." Her face turned in his hand and she kissed his palm. "You stole my heart. I'm going to have to be less mousy librarian and more reach-for-what-I-want woman and do something about that."

Oh, yeah, that sounded good. "So you will then?" he insisted. "You'll marry me?"

"Silly man, have you forgotten?" his one-time summer romance but now forever-woman asked. "I already did."

* * * * *

*Celebrate 60 years of pure reading
pleasure with Harlequin® Books!*

*Harlequin Romance® is celebrating
by showering you with*
DIAMOND BRIDES
in February 2009.

*Six stories that promise to bring a touch
of sparkle to your life, with diamond proposals
and dazzling weddings, sparkling brides and
gorgeous grooms!*

Enjoy a sneak peek at Caroline Anderson's
TWO LITTLE MIRACLES,
*available February 2009
from Harlequin Romance®.*

'I'VE FOUND HER.'

Max froze.

It was what he'd been waiting for since June, but now—now he was almost afraid to voice the question. His heart stalling, he leaned slowly back in his chair and scoured the investigator's face for clues. 'Where?' he asked, and his voice sounded rough and unused, like a rusty hinge.

'In Suffolk. She's living in a cottage.'

Living. His heart crashed back to life, and he sucked in a long, slow breath. All these months he'd feared—

'Is she well?'

'Yes, she's well.'

He had to force himself to ask the next question. 'Alone?'

The man paused. 'No. The cottage belongs to a man called John Blake. He's working away at the moment, but he comes and goes.'

God. He felt sick. So sick he hardly registered the next few words, but then gradually they sank in. 'She's got *what?*'

'Babies. Twin girls. They're eight months old.'

'Eight—' he echoed under his breath. 'They must be his.'

He was thinking out loud, but the P.I. heard and corrected him.

'Apparently not. I gather they're hers. She's been there since mid-January last year, and they were born during the summer—June, the woman in the post office thought. She was more than helpful. I think there's been a certain amount of speculation about their relationship.'

He'd just bet there had. God, he was going to kill her. Or Blake. Maybe both of them.

'Of course, looking at the dates, she was presumably pregnant when she left you, so they could be yours, or she could have been having an affair with this Blake character before…'

He glared at the unfortunate P.I. 'Just stick to your

job. I can do the math,' he snapped, swallowing the un-palatable possibility that she'd been unfaithful to him before she'd left. 'Where is she? I want the address.'

'It's all in here,' the man said, sliding a large en-velope across the desk to him. 'With my invoice.'

'I'll get it seen to. Thank you.'

'If there's anything else you need, Mr Gallagher, any further information—'

'I'll be in touch.'

'The woman in the post office told me Blake was away at the moment, if that helps,' he added quietly, and opened the door.

Max stared down at the envelope, hardly daring to open it, but when the door clicked softly shut be-hind the P.I., he eased up the flap, tipped it and felt his breath jam in his throat as the photos spilled out over the desk.

Oh, lord, she looked gorgeous. Different, though. It took him a moment to recognise her, because she'd grown her hair, and it was tied back in a ponytail, making her look younger and somehow freer. The blond highlights were gone, and it was back to its natural soft golden brown, with a little curl in the end of the ponytail that he wanted to thread his finger through and tug, just gently, to draw her back to him.

Crazy. She'd put on a little weight, but it suited her. She looked well and happy and beautiful, but oddly, considering how desperate he'd been for news of her for the past year—one year, three weeks and two days, to be exact—it wasn't only Julia who held his attention after the initial shock. It was the babies sitting side by side in a supermarket trolley. Two identical and absolutely beautiful little girls.

* * * * *

When Max Gallagher hires a P.I. to find his estranged wife, Julia, he discovers she's not alone—she has twin baby girls, and they might be his. Now workaholic Max has just two weeks to prove that he can be a wonderful husband and father to the family he wants to treasure.

Look for TWO LITTLE MIRACLES
by Caroline Anderson,
available February 2009
from Harlequin Romance®.

CELEBRATE
60 YEARS
OF PURE READING PLEASURE
WITH HARLEQUIN®!

We'll be spotlighting a different series
every month throughout 2009
to celebrate our 60th anniversary.

Look for Harlequin® Romance in February!

**Harlequin® Romance is celebrating by showering
you with Diamond Brides in February 2009.**

Six stories that promise to bring a touch of sparkle to
your life, with diamond proposals and dazzling weddings,
sparkling brides and gorgeous grooms!

Collect all six books in February 2009,
featuring *Two Little Miracles* by Caroline Anderson.

*Look for the Diamond Brides miniseries
in February 2009!*

www.eHarlequin.com   HRBRIDES09

HARLEQUIN® Romance®

This February the Harlequin® Romance series will feature six Diamond Brides stories featuring diamond proposals and gorgeous grooms.

Share your dream wedding proposal and you could WIN!

The most romantic entry will win a diamond necklace and will inspire a proposal in one of our upcoming Diamond Grooms books in 2010.

In 100 words or less, tell us the most romantic way that you dream of being proposed to.

For more information, and to enter the Diamond Brides Proposal contest, please visit **www.DiamondBridesProposal.com**

Or mail your entry to us at:

IN THE U.S.: 3010 Walden Ave., P.O. Box 9069, Buffalo, NY 14269-9069
IN CANADA: 225 Duncan Mill Road, Don Mills, ON M3B 3K9

You're invited to join our Tell Harlequin Reader Panel!

By joining our new reader panel you will:

- Receive Harlequin® books—they are FREE and yours to keep with no obligation to purchase anything!
- Participate in fun online surveys
- Exchange opinions and ideas with women just like you
- Have a say in our new book ideas and help us publish the best in women's fiction

In addition, you will have a chance to win great prizes and receive special gifts!
See Web site for details. Some conditions apply.
Space is limited.

To join, visit us at
www.TellHarlequin.com.

Tell
HARLEQUIN

REQUEST YOUR FREE BOOKS!

2 FREE NOVELS PLUS 2 FREE GIFTS!

Silhouette®

SPECIAL EDITION®

Life, Love and Family!

YES! Please send me 2 FREE Silhouette Special Edition® novels and my 2 FREE gifts (gifts are worth about $10). After receiving them, if I don't wish to receive any more books, I can return the shipping statement marked "cancel." If I don't cancel, I will receive 6 brand-new novels every month and be billed just $4.24 per book in the U.S. or $4.99 per book in Canada, plus 25¢ shipping and handling per book and applicable taxes, if any*. That's a savings of at least 15% off the cover price! I understand that accepting the 2 free books and gifts places me under no obligation to buy anything. I can always return a shipment and cancel at any time. Even if I never buy another book from Silhouette, the two free books and gifts are mine to keep forever.

235 SDN EEYU   335 SDN EEY6

Name _____ (PLEASE PRINT) _____

Address _____ Apt. # _____

City _____ State/Prov. _____ Zip/Postal Code _____

Signature (if under 18, a parent or guardian must sign)

Mail to the **Silhouette Reader Service:**
IN U.S.A.: P.O. Box 1867, Buffalo, NY 14240-1867
IN CANADA: P.O. Box 609, Fort Erie, Ontario L2A 5X3

Not valid to current subscribers of Silhouette Special Edition books.

Want to try two free books from another line?
Call 1-800-873-8635 or visit www.morefreebooks.com.

* Terms and prices subject to change without notice. N.Y. residents add applicable sales tax. Canadian residents will be charged applicable provincial taxes and GST. Offer not valid in Quebec. This offer is limited to one order per household. All orders subject to approval. Credit or debit balances in a customer's account(s) may be offset by any other outstanding balance owed by or to the customer. Please allow 4 to 6 weeks for delivery. Offer available while quantities last.

Your Privacy: Silhouette is committed to protecting your privacy. Our Privacy Policy is available online at www.eHarlequin.com or upon request from the Reader Service. From time to time we make our lists of customers available to reputable third parties who may have a product or service of interest to you. If you would prefer we not share your name and address, please check here. ☐

SSE08R

#1 *NEW YORK TIMES* BESTSELLING AUTHOR

DEBBIE MACOMBER

How to meet and marry a man in Seattle

There are all the usual ways, of course, but here's how Janine Hartman and Meg Remington did it.

Janine: My grandfather Hartman *arranged* a husband for me! Zach Thomas, the intended groom, was just as outraged as I was. But Gramps insisted we'd be "a perfect match." *First Comes Marriage,* according to him.

Meg: My teenage daughter, Lindsey, had the nerve to place a personal ad on my behalf—*Wanted: Perfect Partner.* Worse, Steve Conlan, who answered the ad, *was* perfect, according to her.

Married in Seattle

*Available the first week of January 2009
wherever books are sold!*

MIRA®

Silhouette®

COMING NEXT MONTH
Available February 24, 2009

#1957 TRIPLE TROUBLE—Lois Faye Dyer
Fortunes of Texas: Return to Red Rock
Financial analyst Nick Fortune was a whiz at numbers, not diapers. So after tragedy forced him to assume guardianship of triplets, he was clueless—until confident Charlene London became their nanny. That's when Nick fell for Charlene, and the trouble really began!

#1958 TRAVIS'S APPEAL—Marie Ferrarella
Kate's Boys
Shana O'Reilly couldn't deny it—family lawyer Travis Marlowe had some kind of appeal. But as Travis handled her father's tricky estate planning, he discovered things weren't what they seemed in the O'Reilly clan. Would an explosive secret leave Travis and Shana's budding relationship in tatters?

#1959 A TEXAN ON HER DOORSTEP—Stella Bagwell
Famous Families
More Famous Families from Special Edition! Abandoned by his mother, shafted by his party-girl ex-wife, cynical Texas lawman Mac McCleod was over love. Until a chance reunion with his mother in a hospital, and a choice introduction to her intriguing doctor, Ileana Murdock, changed everything....

#1960 MARRYING THE VIRGIN NANNY—Teresa Southwick
The Nanny Network
Billionaire Jason Garrett would pay a premium to the Nanny Network for a caregiver for his infant son, Brady. And luckily, sweet, innocent nanny Maggie Shepherd instantly bonded with father and son, giving Jason a priceless new lease on love.

#1961 LULLABY FOR TWO—Karen Rose Smith
The Baby Experts
When Vince Rossi assumed custody of his friend's baby son after an accident, the little boy was hurt, and if it weren't for Dr. Tessa McGuire, Vince wouldn't know which end was up. Sure, Tessa was Vince's ex-wife and they had a rocky history, but as they bonded over the boy, could it be they had a future—together—too?

#1962 CLAIMING THE RANCHER'S HEART—Cindy Kirk
Footloose Stacie Collins had a knack for matchmaking. After inheriting her grandma's home in Montana, she and two gal pals decided to head for the hills and test their theories of love on the locals. When their "scientific" survey yielded Josh Collins as Stacie's ideal beau, it must have been a computer error—or was this rugged rancher really a perfect match?

SSECNMBPA0209